ACCABADORA

1950s Sardinia. When Tzia Bonaria adopts Maria, an unloved fourth child, she tries to shield the girl from the truth about her role as an accabadora, an angel of mercy who acts as a midwife to the dying. Moved by the pleas of a young man crippled in an accident, Bonaria breaks her golden rule of familial consent; and in the recriminations that follow, Maria rejects Tzia Bonaria and flees Sardinia for Turin. Adrift in the big city, she strives to find love and acceptance, but her efforts are overshadowed by the creeping knowledge of a debt unpaid and of a destiny that must one day be hers . . .

SP... ...L MESSAGE TO READERS

IH... ...VERSCROFT FOUNDATION
re... ...d UK charity number 264873)
as... ...shed in 1972 to provide funds for
ar... ...gnosis and treatment of eye diseases.
I... ...es of major projects funded by
... ...Ulverscroft Foundation are:-

...ldren's Eye Unit at Moorfields Eye
... London

...erscroft Children's Eye Unit at Great
... Street Hospital for Sick Children

... research into eye diseases and
...t at the Department of Ophthalmology,
...y of Leicester

...verscroft Vision Research Group,
...of Child Health

...erating theatres at the Western
...ic Hospital, London

...ir of Ophthalmology at the Royal
...1 College of Ophthalmologists

... further the work of the Foundation
... g a donation or leaving a legacy.
... ntribution is gratefully received. If you
would like to help support the Foundation or
require further information, please contact:

THE ULVERSCROFT FOUNDATION
The Green, Bradgate Road, Anstey
Leicester LE7 7FU, England
Tel: (0116) 236 4325

website: www.foundation.ulverscroft.com

Michela Murgia was born in Cabras, Sardinia, in 1972. As a young Italian writer, Murgia has a strong social networking presence, with thousands of Facebook fans. Her online blog inspired the screenplay for the 2008 Italian film *Whole World Ahead*. *Accabadora* is Murgia's English-language debut (having been translated by Silvester Mazzarella), and it has won seven major literary prizes, including Italy's prestigious Premio Campiello.

MICHELA MURGIA

◆

ACCABADORA

Complete and Unabridged

ULVERSCROFT
Leicester

First published in Great Britain in 2011 by
MacLehose Press
an imprint of
Quercus
London

First Large Print Edition
published 2014
by arrangement with
Quercus
London

A catalogue record for this book is available
from the British Library.

ISBN 978–1–4448–2040–9

Published by
F. A. Thorpe (Publishing)
Anstey, Leicestershire

Set by Words & Graphics Ltd.
Anstey, Leicestershire
Printed and bound in Great Britain by
T. J. International Ltd., Padstow, Cornwall

This book is printed on acid-free paper

To my mother.
Both of them.

GLOSSARY

abbardente	highly alcoholic, transparent spirit, sometimes flavoured with wild fennel or arbutus berry
amaretto	small cake or biscuit made with bitter almonds
aranzada	softened orange peel with honey, almonds and sugar
attittadora	woman paid to attend funerals to pray and cry
babbo	dad, father
capigliette	filled pastry with almonds and lemon
culurgiones	small pasta envelopes filled with potatoes, cheese, spices, etc. and served with tomato sauce and grated pecorino cheese
gueffus	balls of almond paste
mistral	strong, cold wind coming from the north or northwest
nuraghe	Bronze Age structure from the Nuragic civilization particular to Sardinia, a truncated conical tower of stone resembling a beehive

pabassinos	small cakes with either sultanas (*uva sultanina*) or raisins (*uva secca*)
pirichittus	filled pastry containing lemon
saba	a kind of molasses or treacle made with grape must or prickly pear
tiliccas	filled pastry with *saba*, almonds, spices and grated orange or lemon peel
tzia/tzio	aunt/uncle

1

Fill'e anima: soul-child.

That is what they call children who are
conceived twice, from the poverty of one
woman and the sterility of another. Maria
Listru became such a child, late fruit of the
soul of Bonaria Urrai.

When the old woman stopped under the
lemon tree to speak to the child's mother,
Anna Teresa Listru, Maria was six years old, a
mistake after three things done right. With
her sisters already grown into young ladies,
she was playing alone in the dirt, making a
mud tart full of live ants with the attentive
care of a young housewife. The ants died
slowly, waving their reddish legs under the
decoration of wild flowers and sand masquer-
ading as sugar. Under the fierce July sun
Maria's pudding grew in her hands with the
beauty that sometimes characterizes evil
things. Looking up from the mud, the little
girl saw Tzia Bonaria Urrai smiling beside
her, backlit against the bright sun, her hands
resting on her meagre stomach which had
just been filled by an offering from Anna

Maria Listru. Maria would not understand the significance of that offering until much later.

Still, she went off with Tzia Bonaria that very day, carrying her mud tart in one hand and in the other, her mother's pitiful final gesture to see her on her way, a bag of fresh eggs and parsley.

Maria was smiling. She felt intuitively that there must be a reason to cry, but she could not quite remember what it was. And already, as they left, she was finding it difficult to remember her birth-mother's face, as if she had forgotten it long ago, in that mysterious moment when a young girl first makes up her mind what will be the best ingredients for her own mud tart. But she did remember that hot sky for many years and the feet of Tzia Bonaria in her sandals, one slipping out under the hem of her black skirt as the other was hidden by it, in a silent dance whose rhythm Maria's own legs had difficulty in following

Tzia Bonaria gave her a bed all to herself in a room full of saints, all nasty ones. Thus did Maria learn that paradise is no place for children. Two nights she lay awake, silent, eyes wide open in the darkness, expecting to see tears of blood or sparks fly from haloes. On the third night she gave way to her terror of the sacred heart with the finger pointed at it, made even more alarming by the three heavy rosaries that hung amid the blood spurting from the chest. She could take it no longer, and cried out.

Tzia Bonaria, opening the door a few seconds later, found Maria standing by the wall hugging the shaggy wool pillow she had chosen as her comfort-blanket. She looked next at the bleeding statue which seemed to be nearer the bed than ever. She carried it away under her arm without a word, and next day the holy-water bowl with a picture of Santa Rita inside it disappeared from the dresser, and so did the mystical plaster lamb, curly like a dog but as ferocious as a lion. It took a while for Maria to begin reciting the *Ave* again, and even then she did it very softly for fear the Madonna might hear and take her seriously in the hour of our death amen.

★ ★ ★

It was hard to guess Tzia Bonaria's age in those days; she seemed ageless, immutable, frozen in time, as though she had suddenly decided for herself to be much older than her calendar years and was now patiently waiting for time to catch up. Whereas Maria, arriving too late into her mother's womb, had always known she was the last concern in a family already weighed down with cares. But now, in the house of this woman, she began to experience the unfamilar feeling that she mattered. She knew, when she set off for school in the morning, holding tight her textbook, that she had only to turn to see her benefactor standing watching her, leaning against the frame of the door as if holding it up.

Maria was not aware of it, but it was especially at night that the old woman came close to her, on ordinary nights when the little girl had no sin to blame for keeping her awake. Tzia Bonaria would come silently into the room and sit down by the sleeping child's bed, gazing at her in the darkness. Meanwhile, imagining herself first in the thoughts of Bonaria Urrai, Maria would sleep, untroubled as yet by the knowledge that she was unique.

It was perfectly clear to the people of Soreni why Anna Teresa Listru had given her youngest daughter to the old woman. Ignoring the advice of her family, she had married the wrong man, simply to spend the next fifteen years grumbling that he had shown himself able to do only one thing well. Anna Teresa Listru loved to complain to her neighbours that her husband had been

4

useless even in death since he had not even had the grace to snuff it in the war so as to leave her with a pension. Rejected as unfit for military service because he was so small, Sisinnio Listru had died as stupidly as he had lived, squashed like a pressed grape under the tractor of Boreddu Arresi, for whom he had worked from time to time as a share tenant. As a widow with four daughters, Anna Teresa Listru had dwindled from being poor to being destitute and learning, as she often was heard to say, to make stew with the shadow of the church bell. But now that Tzia Bonaria had asked if she could take Maria as her own daughter, it was almost beyond Anna Teresa's wildest dreams that she could add a couple of potatoes grown on the Urrai property to her soup every day. The fact that her youngest child was the price she paid for this privilege was of little concern to her; after all, she still had three others.

But no-one had the slightest idea why Tzia Bonaria Urrai at her age should have wanted to take another woman's daughter into her home. The silences lengthened like shadows when the old woman and the child passed down the road together, provoking whispered fragments of gossip among those sitting on the village benches. Bainzu, the tobacconist, was inspired to say that even the well-off, when they grew old, needed a second pair of hands to help wipe their bums. But Luciana Lodine, grown-up daughter of the plumber, could not understand why anyone should need to take on an heir to do what any well-paid servant could do. And Ausonia Frau, who knew more about bums than any nurse, would cap the discussion by declaring that not even vixens liked to die alone, and after this no-one had anything more to add.

Of course it was true that, had not Bonaria Urrai been born into a wealthy family, she would have ended up no different from any other female without a man, let alone have been able to take on a *fill'e anima*. The widow of a husband who had never married her, she would perhaps in a different station of life have been a whore, or have lived out the rest of her life dressed in black behind closed shutters in monastic seclusion either at home or in a convent. She had lost her wedding-dress to the war, even if some did not believe that Raffaele Zincu had really died on the Piave: perhaps he had been crafty enough to find another woman up there and save himself the trouble and expense of the journey home. Perhaps this was why Bonaria Urrai had become old even when still young, and why no night ever seemed blacker to Maria than Bonaria's skirt. But all the local

6

gossips knew the district was full of 'widows' whose husbands were still alive, and Bonaria Urrai knew it too, which was why she would walk with her head held high and would never stop to talk to anyone but go straight home stiff as a rhymed verse after going out each morning to collect her new-baked bread.

For Bonaria the most difficult thing about her decision to take a *fill'e anima* was by no means the curiosity of others, rather it was the initial reaction of the child she had taken into her home. After six years sharing the air of a single room each night with three sisters, it was natural for Maria to believe her own private space could never extend further than the length of her arm. Coming into the house of Bonaria Urrai had caused a major upheaval in the little girl's interior geography, now that she was living between walls where the spaces she could think of as her own were so ample that it took her several weeks to realize that no-one would come out from behind the doors of the many closed rooms to say, 'Don't touch, that's mine.' But Bonaria Urrai never made the mistake of pressing Maria to treat the house as her own; she never used any of those conventional clichés that only serve to remind guests that they are most certainly not in their own homes. Bonaria preferred to wait until those spaces left empty for years gradually adjusted themselves to the little girl's presence and, when within a month all the rooms had been opened and were left open, she felt she had been right to let the house look after itself. As soon as Maria felt strong in the new confidence she had developed within those walls, she gradually began to show more curiosity about the woman who had brought her there to live.

'Whose daughter are you, Tzia?' she said one day through a mouthful of soup.

'My father's name was Taniei Urrai, that gentleman over there.'

Bonaria pointed at the faded brown photograph hanging over the fireplace, in which Daniele Urrai, standing stiffly in a velvet waistcoat at the age of about thirty looked to the little girl like anything but the father of the old woman in front of her. Bonaria read the disbelief in Maria's rosy face.

'Of course he was young then, I hadn't even been born,' she said.

'Didn't you have any *mamma*?' said Maria, who was clearly unfamiliar with the idea that it was possible to be the daughter of a father.

'Of course I did, she was called Anna. But she too died many years ago.'

'Like my father,' Maria said seriously.

'Sometimes they do that.'

Bonaria was astonished at her clarification. 'What?'

'They do that. They die before we are born.' Maria gave Bonaria a patient look. Then she forced herself to add: 'Rita told me, Angelo Muntoni's daughter. Her *papà* died before she was born too.'

As she explained, she waved her spoon in the air like a violinist his bow.

'Yes, some do. But not all,' said Bonaria, watching her with a vague smile.

'Oh no, not all,' said Maria. 'One at least has to stay alive. For the children. That's why you always have two parents.'

Bonaria nodded, dipping her spoon into her soup in the belief that the conversation was at an end.

'And there were two of you?'

It took Bonaria a moment to understand. Then she went on eating, and spoke again in the same almost casual tone.

'Yes, we were two. My husband's dead as well.'

'Oh. He's dead . . . ' Maria said after a short pause, uncertain whether to be relieved or sorry.

'Yes,' Bonaria said, serious in her turn. 'Sometimes they do that.'

Comforted by this personal revelation, the

little girl went back to blowing on her soup. Every now and then, looking up through the steam from her spoon, she found herself meeting Tzia Bonaria's eyes and could not help smiling.

After that, whenever Bonaria went out in the morning to buy the bread, Maria would sit at the kitchen table swinging her feet, silently counting the number of times her rubber shoes hit the chair. After about three hundred, Tzia Bonaria would be back, and before Maria went off to school they would be able to enjoy some warm bread with baked figs.

'Eat, Maria, so your titties can grow!' Tzia would say, tapping the meagre remnants of her own breasts with her hand.

Maria would laugh and cram two figs into her mouth at once, then run into her room with seeds still stuck between her teeth to check, because everything Tzia Bonaria said was God's law on earth. Yet in all the thirteen years they shared a home, Maria never once called her '*Mamma*', because mothers are something different.

2

For some time Maria thought that Tzia Bonaria was a seamstress. She would spend hours at a time sewing, and one of the rooms was always full of remnants and pieces of cloth. Women would come to be measured for skirts and headscarves, and men sometimes for trousers and formal shirts. Tzia Bonaria would never allow the men into the room where she kept her cloth, but received them in the sitting-room where they had to remain standing. She would crawl about on her knees with her tape measure like a female spider, rapidly weaving a mysterious web of measurements round her immobile prey.

The women, while they were being measured, would chatter about their own lives while pretending to discuss the lives of others. The men on the other hand kept quiet, gloomy and as if naked, faced by those extraordinarily precise eyes. Maria would watch and ask questions.

'It embarrasses men to be measured because you're a woman, doesn't it?'

At this Bonaria Urrai would give her a cunning look that contrasted strangely with the studied severity of her face.

'Good heavens, Mariedda! They aren't embarrassed, they're scared. They know what sort of a coat they might get from me.' Then she would laugh gently and give the cloth a sharp shake to stretch it.

Scared or not, the men would even come from as far away as Illamari and Luvè, before weddings or saints' days, or just for a new Sunday suit. Sometimes the house was like a market, with metres of cloth hung over the backs of chairs, perhaps material for skirts or embroidery. Maria would sit and watch, ready to hand Bonaria a needle or a piece of chalk to mark the length of a hem. Once, wanting a pair of trousers, no less a figure than Boriccu Silai from the mining consortium came, together with his domestic servant. The girl must have been about sixteen; her name was Annagrazia and she had a pockmarked face and eyes like snails without their shells. She stood in silence by the wall, holding a package with at least four metres of smooth velvet, something only really rich people could afford. Tzia Bonaria was not at all intimidated and continued to measure Boriccu Silai with her usual care, noting his shape below the belt with the expert eye of one who needs very little information to understand a great deal.

Finally, eyeing his flies, she asked with the air of a meticulous tailor, 'Which side do you dress?' He gestured with his head to the girl leaning against the wall.

'The left,' Annagrazia answered for her employer, staring at the old woman without further explanation. Bonaria held the servant's eyes for a moment, then slowly began rewinding her leather tape measure round its lemon-wood stick. Boriccu waited, but when Tzia Bonaria spoke again she no longer seemed to be addressing him.

'Well, I'm sorry but I won't be able to get the job done by St Ignazio's day. Try Rosa Cadinu, she needs the work.'

Boricco Silai and Tzia Bonaria stood still, summing each other up in silence. Then the man and his intimate servant left the house without another word; more than enough had already been said. Tzia Bonaria carefully shut the door behind them, then turned to Maria with a tired sigh and replaced her tape measure in the pocket of her well-used overall.

'To hell with them, a job lost . . . but with some things it's better not to know the exact measurements, Maria. Do you follow me?'

Maria had not understood anything at all but nodded all the same, because you cannot always expect to understand everything you hear the minute you hear it. In any case, she was still under the impression that Tzia Bonaria worked as a seamstress.

★ ★ ★

The first time Maria noticed Tzia Bonaria go out at night was just after Epiphany, in the the winter of 1955, when she was eight years old. She had been allowed to stay up and play until the *Ave Maria* sounded, then Tzia Bonaria had taken her to her room for an early night, closing the shutters and refilling the open warming-pan with embers and hot ashes.

'Now go to sleep. It's up early tomorrow for school.'

Maria hardly ever paid much attention to this parody of night-time, sometimes lying awake for hours watching the shadows cast by the dying embers on the ceiling.

On this occasion she was still awake when she heard a knock on the front door, and the hushed though emotional voice of a man speaking too quietly for her to recognize him. Keeping still under the bedclothes in the light of the glowing embers, she heard the unmistakable sound of the courtyard gate opening and Tzia Bonaria's familiar step going out and coming back a few minutes later. Getting out of bed and oblivious of the cold floor against her bare feet, Maria groped her way towards the door but accidentally kicked her chamber pot in the darkness. Even before she came out of her room, Tzia knew she was awake.

'The child!' the man said in a low voice from the shadows of the hall. He was tall and broad-shouldered and his face was vaguely familiar, but Maria had no time to identify him because Tzia was instantly before her, black and severe in the long woollen shawl she only wore when she went out to keep appointments. The shawl enclosed her lean body as tightly as a jewel-case, concealing both her figure and her intentions, whatever they may have been.

'Go back to your room.'

Maria could not see her face, perhaps the reason she had the courage to ask questions.

'Where are you going, Tzia? What's happening?'

'I'll be back soon. But you go to your room.'

It was a command, and had already been given once more than strictly necessary, and in front of a stranger at that. Maria backed silently into the narrow opening of her door. Until she closed it, the old woman stayed motionless, forcing her caller to do the same.

On the other side of the door Maria held her breath like a secret, until she heard them move quickly again, going out and leaving the house unnaturally silent. Stupefied by the cold, she followed her usual routine and tapped her finger softly on the wooden door-jamb to count, but by around three times a hundred Bonaria Urrai had still not come back. Resigned, the little girl went back to bed in wide-awake silence, until despite everything the warmth in the room lulled her to sleep. When the old woman did come back, Maria was asleep and did not notice. Which was just as well.

In the morning the familiar sounds of the household woke her. The questions of the night had proved as evanescent as the smell from the dying embers. She dressed and went to look for Tzia, finding her shaking out a piece of cloth in the air, to free it of dust and stretch its threadbare texture, like a bird with just one wing. When Bonaria saw Maria she stopped, then spoke.

'What you did last night must never happen again.'

The command reached Maria as sharply as a whiplash of cloth, suppressing all questions with its menace. Maria understood then and there that she stood to lose something more precious than her sleep. Then the old woman's face relaxed, and she folded away the piece of cloth and said:

'Eat now, because we've a lot to do today.'

She dressed Maria in her little party dress and put on her own best mourning skirt even though it was a Tuesday with no religious obligations. She plaited her grey hair with her eyes fixed on the windowpane while the shadows wove a subtle texture on her face. Among the folds of skirt and womanhood Maria for the first time became aware of a departed beauty, and felt sad there was no longer anyone to remember it.

'Where are we going, Tzia?'

The old woman put on her blackest headscarf, the silk one with the long fringe that constantly got into knots. Then she turned to the little girl with a strange expression on her dry face.

'We must pay a mourning call at the house of Rachela Littorra, who's lost her husband. It's our duty as neighbours.'

★   ★   ★

The old woman walked at her usual speed and beside her Maria had to struggle to keep up, even though her little white dress was much lighter than the old woman's long heavy skirt. It was not far to the dead man's

17

house, but the sombre tones of the formal lament could already be heard from a few hundred metres away. Each time the rough music of the lament came through, it was as if every household were singing of its sorrows to the people of Soreni, both sorrows of the present and sorrows of the past, because the mourning of any one family reawakened the still-sensitive memory of every single lamentation that had gone before. This was why the neighbourhood shutters were half-closed to shield the eyes of the houses from the sun, as everyone hurried to mourn their own dead vicariously through this latest death.

The dead man of the moment lay stretched on a bed in the middle of the entrance hall, his shod feet pointing towards the front door. They had already dressed him for burial as if for a party, in the best suit he had worn to be married when he was slim and healthy and had life under control. The buttons were strained across his stomach even with his body stretched out, and the atmosphere was heavy with the broken breathing of women, while the men stood motionless against the wall as if on guard. The official principal mourner or *attittadora* launched into a sing-song lament, a grieving note that seemed to emerge from deep down where her knees bent against the floor. The women echoed her with rhythmic moans, creating a lugubrious chorus that Tzia Bonaria made no attempt to join. Telling Maria to wait, she went up to the widow Rachela Littorra, who was huddled on the chair nearest to the dead man's head, rocking herself in silence while the other women did her lamenting for her. When she saw Tzia Bonaria she seemed to rouse herself, getting to her feet in a gesture of welcome.

'Highly esteemed sister! May God repay you for everything . . . '

For a moment her words rose above the professional lament of the mourners. Then the rest of what she had to say was lost in Tzia Bonaria's black wool shawl, where the widow buried her face in a surge of uncontrolled emotion, attracting the attention of the onlookers. Rachela Littorra seemed to recover her control a little only when Tzia whispered something to her, touching her head lightly with a grace Maria had never seen in her before.

The *attittadora* had meanwhile changed her note, intoning an improvised poem in praise of the dead man. To hear her shrieking in rhyme you would imagine no better man than Giacomo Littorra had ever lived, whereas everyone knew he had been a stingy husband who believed that virtue consisted in being as pitiless towards everyone else as he believed destiny had been to him. While the hired mourners wept and pretended to rip their sleeves with their teeth, Maria could read this inadmissable thought on the faces of those present, scarcely lifting her eyes as she glanced from one to another.

It was then that she recognized him, the man.

Standing against the wall behind his mother's chair and holding his hat in his hand, the son of the dead man was the tallest man present. Santino Littorra's eyes were fixed on the rigid body of his father, as if hypnotized by the sounds of grief simulated by the professional mourners. Maria recognized the broad shoulders and the controlled and patient manner of the night before. Eight years were too few to understand everything, but they were enough for her to know intuitively that there was more to understand. Returning home less than two hours later, Maria walked as slowly as if carrying a burden, but it was perhaps the last time she dragged behind Tzia Bonaria on the road.

3

For five years Bonaria Urrai did not go out again at night, or if she did Maria was not aware of it, busy learning her place as a legitimate daughter. Somehow her unusual relationship with Tzia Bonaria worked, because by the time she reached her final year at primary school it had long been accepted by the people of Soreni; it was no longer the subject of conversation in the bars, and even during doorstep conversations at dusk the subject of the old woman and the child had been replaced by more recent and more dramatic news. Without realizing what a useful contribution she was making in this respect, the sixteen-year-old daughter of Rosanna Sinai had been so considerate as to become pregnant by a man as yet unknown, a godsend to the local gossips. Anyone but Bonaria Urrai, once the murmur of rumours behind her back had ceased, would have been astonished that the subject had been dropped so quickly because in places where little of real interest ever happens, an event of this kind can remain newsworthy for a generation. But Bonaria could not have been surprised, because she had worked so hard from the first to create that fragile normality. The elderly seamstress had always treated the child like the fruit of her own womb, allowing her the freedom of the house when people came to call, and taking her wherever she went, so that everyone was free to stuff themselves with insatiable curiosity until it was coming out of their ears as far as the nature of her elective motherhood was concerned. On the other hand, Maria, used to thinking herself profoundly insignificant, had found it more difficult to accept that she had become important. Her birth mother, Anna Teresa Listru, loved numbers, and had always fallen back on a ritual formula to teach Maria her place in a series of sisters:

'And who is this pretty child?'

'Oh, she's my last,' Or, 'She's the fourth.'

So powerful had been the influence of this racecourse classification on Maria that at first she had had to bite her tongue so as not to present herself automatically as the fourth or last. Bonaria could not have known this but must in some way have intuited it because, when she had to introduce Maria to strangers, she would always speak before they could ask anything:

'This is Maria.'

And that she was simply Maria had to be

enough for everyone, including those who were dying to know more. It took a little time for the people of Soreni to grasp this, but in the end they came to accept the antiphony of that mysterious liturgy, and suddenly it was as if it had always been that way: a soul and the child of that soul, a less guilty way of being mother and daughter. Only once did anyone look for a more ample explanation from Bonaria, and in many ways that single episode affected everything that came after.

★ ★ ★

The children of 5B found it hard to believe that their teacher, Maestra Luciana, was really fifty because she was too beautiful to be old, and beautiful in that dangerous way only found in women from the outside world. She had long been married to Giuseppe Meli, a Soreni landowner who specialized in growing rice and who often travelled to the continent to arrange deals connected with the export of the Sardinian arboreal variety. This was how Giuseppe had come to meet his wife, a slim girl of middle-class Piedmontese stock, a well-mannered young teacher with jade-green eyes, uncommon even in the girls of the world she came from, where strings of pearls abounded. Luciana Tellani had surprised her

23

family and friends by agreeing to follow Giuseppe Meli without so much as a backward glance, but even though she had now been teaching at Soreni for more than twenty years, she still spoke the Italian of Turin. During this time she had taught many to read and write, and they in return had silently and completely accepted her as one of themselves, with the gratitude and respect modest people often feel for good teachers. The foreigner who in the late forties had married the farmer Giuseppe Meli, was now known at Soreni simply as Maestra Luciana.

Her still youthful fair hair barely reached her shoulders and she never covered her head even in church, where her blonde head stood out among the rest like a poppy in a cornfield. Even so, the worst that could ever be said against her was that being a continental she was much taller than the average for the neighbourhood, and if she also happened to be blonde, well, secondary defects like her height could easily be forgiven, even at Soreni. What Maria particularly liked about her teacher's hair was that she wore it loose. Not smoothly plastered against her head like the fur of a mouse that had fallen into the olive oil, or curly like her birth-mother's hair, which was so convoluted you could never get your hands through it. There was a softness in Maestra

Luciana'a hair that responded to every least breath of wind.

'Maestra, do you press your hair with a hot iron to get it like that?'

'The very idea, Maria! How would I ever have time to curl my hair each morning with you lot waiting for me in the classroom!'

The teacher liked this girl with her slightly impudent intelligence, and was happy to accept her unusual family background, assisted by clarifications from her husband and one or two of those simple souls always anxious to explain the more complicated lives of others. But a little tension had been caused by the failure of Bonaria Urrai to turn up to any of the meetings the teacher tried to arrange with her. When the girl brought home her exercise book with a written request from Maestra Luciana, Tzia Bonaria gave her a sharp look.

'What have you been up to?'

'Nothing!' Maria said, untying the green bow on her school uniform.

'Then why does the teacher want to see me?'

'I don't know.'

'You must have done something, or she wouldn't be asking to see me.'

'I haven't done anything, and I'm getting on fine at school too: I got 'Excellent' for geometry yesterday!'

Bonaria helped her off with her black school overall and said nothing more, but next day she dressed as for a formal occasion and went to see Maestra Luciana. She knocked on the classroom door at the specified time, and a few seconds later the two women were face to face, the teacher in a blue tailor-made houndstooth suit of the kind women wore in the city, and the seamstress in her traditional long skirt with a black shawl round her shoulders. They were scarcely ten years apart in age, but they looked as if they had been born in different generations. Leaving the caretaker to keep an eye on the other children, Maestra Luciana took Bonaria into the corridor.

'You worry me. Has Maria been up to something?' Bonaria said.

'No, not at all. I only asked you to come because I wanted to meet you; it's normal for teacher and parents to meet occasionally to exchange their impressions of a child's progress.'

If Bonaria noticed a very slight hesitation in the voice of the Piedmontese woman, she kept it to herself.

'Well, if that's all it is, here I am. How is Maria getting on?'

'Very well, she's intelligent and works hard. She likes school, maths especially, and gets

26

her homework done on time. Do you supervise her work at home?'

'Not always. Sometimes I'm too busy, and sometimes she's doing things even I can't understand. I only reached third grade in elementary school, you know; I never did much studying.'

Anyone else would have blushed to make such an admission. But Bonaria looked fearlessly into the other woman's eyes, and curiously enough it was the teacher who felt a need to justify herself in some way.

'Yes of course, but you know, sometimes it doesn't mean very much how many years someone spent at school; in the third grade of elementary school they used to do as much Latin as they do today in the fifth grade of grammar school.'

The two went out into the garden that surrounded the school and walked among the flowerbeds, entirely engrossed in each other. Bonaria darted quick direct looks at the teacher while Luciana restricted herself to an occasional glance at the sharp profile of the other woman when she thought herself unobserved.

'It's strange, you know, this business of being a 'child of the soul' . . . '

'What's strange about it?' Bonaria's voice was expressionless.

'Maria does not seem to have been affected by it. Does she often see her birth family?'

'Yes, whenever she asks to. Why should she feel resentment?'

Luciana Tellani answered at once, as if she had already been thinking the matter over for a long time to be ready for the day the old woman should come for their interview.

'I don't know, just that it surprises me, for example, that when I ask her to draw a picture of her parents, Maria always draws you and not her real mother.'

Bonaria showed no surprise at this revelation, leaving a silence so that the other, embarrassed, felt a need to go on.

'Well, it seems to me rather strange that a little girl should be taken away . . . with consent of course, but anyway, that she should be taken away from her family in this way, without showing any signs of trauma.'

'There's nothing strange about it, it happens from time to time in this district. If you go to Gennari you'll find at least three soul-children, one of them a girl of about Maria's age.' Bonaria stopped to let the idea sink in. 'It's not strange at all.'

The Piedmontese woman did not seem convinced, but said no more. She let the conversation move on to the child's less brilliant academic achievements, and when

28

they got back to the door of the classroom the teacher indicated that the interview was at an end. But Bonaria had one last question for her.

'I wanted to ask you, about Maria's drawings . . . what exactly did you mean when you said she never draws her real mother?'

The teacher was dumbfounded, more by the expression on the face of the elderly seamstress than by her words.

'Please don't misunderstand me, I was referring to her natural mother; of course I have no wish to interfere in her relationship with you.'

'For Maria, her natural mother is the one she draws when people ask her to draw her mother.'

Perhaps it was the old woman's tone, so light and calm. Or perhaps her expressionless look, as if she were looking through the teacher. Whatever the reason, Maestra Luciana felt it wiser to say no more, tightening her lips into the rigid parody of a smile. The two women parted in a silence weighted with ambivalent tension: one sorry not to have said more at the exact point where the other was convinced she had heard more than enough.

That evening before supper Bonaria switched on the radio, while Maria sat in front of the fire playing with an old shape-sorter puzzle, carefully fitting the cut-out pictures into the right slots. A few were missing, lost during her first years at school, when the objects and their names were still mysteries as yet undefined by the subtle violence of logical analysis.

'What did the teacher want to say?'

'Nothing much, you were quite right.'

'But you spent a long time with her.'

'We looked round the garden. She has some streaked geraniums hidden away there that I'd never seen before.'

Maria slotted the final pieces into their places, aware that whatever Tzia and the teacher had been discussing, she was not going to be able to find out what it was by direct questioning.

'But did she say I'm doing alright?'

'No, she said for a child as intelligent as you, you don't work hard enough and could do much better.'

The little girl stared in disbelief. Bonaria seemed deeply serious, her ear to the classical music coming from the radio, her eyes closed against Maria's inquisitive gaze.

'That can't be right. She always tells me I'm doing well. Best of the class!'

'The best in the class is Giovanni Lai's daughter, everyone in the village knows that. The teacher says you spend all your time

30

drawing and don't like grammar and never stop chattering with Andría Bastíu.'

'It's not true I spend all my time drawing! Only a bit!'

Bonaria gave an imperceptible smile.

'But it's true you chatter and don't study your grammar properly.'

'Anyway, the Italian language is no use.'

'How do you mean it's no use?'

'Outside school we all speak Sard. You do too, and so do my sisters, and Andría. Everyone!'

The old seamstress was quite aware of the common dislike of the Soreni children for the Italian language; every mother in the village knew of that. Some mothers had even stopped speaking Sard to their children for that reason, tackling the new language with results often more comic than effective.

'Even if everyone here understands you when you speak Sard, you still need Italian because in this life you can never know. After all, Sardinia's part of Italy.'

'It's not part of Italy, we're separate from Italy! I've seen that on the map. There's the sea in between,' said Maria confidently.

Bonaria was not going to let herself be wrong-footed by a display of geographical knowledge.

'Maria, whose daughter are you?'

The little girl was taken by surprise. She hesitated, looking for a trap in the question, then planted her feet on firm ground.

'I'm the daughter of Anna Teresa and Sisinnio Listru.'

'Quite right. And where do you live?'

This time Maria saw the trap and paused before answering.

'I live at Soreni.'

'Maria,' said Bonaria, lifting her eyebrows. The little girl was forced to give in.

'I live here with you, Tzia.'

'So you live separate from your mother, but you are still her daughter. Isn't that so? You don't live together, but you are still mother and daughter.'

Maria was silent, mortified, and looked down at the puzzle, in which each piece had its own special place and would fit no other. Her whisper came as light as a puff of air.

'We are mother and daughter, yes . . . but not really a family. If we'd been a family she would never have come to an arrangement with you . . . I mean, I think of you as my family. Because you and I are closer.'

This time it was Bonaria who was silent for a moment. The classical music still coming from the radio did nothing to drown the silence. When she spoke again, she tried a different tack.

32

'It makes me happy to hear you say that, but it doesn't alter the facts . . . because you know very well that my Arrafiei died in the war in the trenches of the Piave. And it was Italy that fought that war, not Sardinia. When someone dies for a country, that country becomes their own. No-one dies for a country that is not his own, unless he's stupid.'

Maria had no weapon against this logic, nor any consolation to offer for a grief so strong as to be still so powerful after forty years. She could see it shining like a light in Bonaria's eyes, the only grave where the lost/believed-missing Raffaele Zincu had never stopped being mourned. In confusion she murmured:

'What are you trying to say, Tzia . . . that I can never be your real daughter till I'm dead?'

Bonaria burst out laughing, breaking the tension so unashamedly revealed in Maria's question. Instinctively she pressed the little girl's head against her lap as if to warm it.

'You silly girl, Mariedda Listru! You became my daughter the very moment I first saw you, when you didn't even yet know who I was. But you must study Italian properly; I ask this of you as a favour to me.'

'Why, Tzia?'

'Because Arrafiei went up into the snows of

33

the Piave in useless light shoes, and unlike him, you must be ready. Italy or no Italy, you must come back safely from the wars, my daughter.'

Bonaria had never called Maria daughter before, nor would she ever do so again in quite the same way. But the intense pleasure Maria felt, as powerful as a pain in the mouth, stayed with her for a long time.

4

If it is true that the land speaks for the people who own it, then the hills round Soreni must have given rise to some very complicated conversations. The tiny, irregular subdivisions told of families with too many children and no common sense, their properties defined by a myriad of contours built from dry walls of black basalt, each carrying its own particular resentment.

The Bastíu family property was just a little bigger than those of its neighbours, since over the years, thanks to God's grace, it had seen more wills than heirs.

At ten o'clock one warm morning in October, in the hillside vineyard known as Pran'e boe, the hand of Andría Bastíu landed clumsily on Maria's slender wrist, arresting the movement of her shears.

'Mind where you put your hand!'

'Why, what's wrong?'

'The web of a poisonous black widow.'

'I'm not scared of spiders.'

'Because you know nothing about them,' said Andría seriously. 'Do you realize that if a black widow bites you, they'll have to bury you in dung and make women dance round you in groups of seven, first widows, then spinsters, and finally married women, till they discover the spider?'

'Where did you get that nonsense, Andrí?' Maria said, laughing as she cut off a large bunch of grapes and arranged it carefully in their plastic bucket, at the same time shaking her head in its headscarf patterned with yellow flowers, faded during earlier vintages.

The Bastíu family vineyard contained two thousand vines heavy with dark grapes the size of quails' eggs. When crushed, they produced a black juice of a consistent sweetness that looked like boiled pig's blood. The two youngsters had divided the work between them in relation to their strength, competing for speed with a parallel line of adults.

'No, I warn you, it's true. When my dad was young it happened to him. He told me if they hadn't made him sweat for two hours under a little mountain of shit, he would have been done for.'

'Wasn't it your dad who died twice in the war? While as for you, if they sent you out to buy a load of nothing in the form of dust, I bet you'd go and do it.'

Maria went on cropping the grapes, teasing Andría with her lively dancing eyes. The boy blushed in the sun, looking down at the pail which was almost full. They were about the same age but Maria, an adult smile on her lips red with grape-juice, had a special gift for finding words to make Andría feel small.

'I'll go and empty the pail into the cart.'

'O.K., off you go then, and I'll find myself something to drink. But beware of the black widow, because if I have to find seven mad women to dance on cowshit to save your life, I'm not at all sure I'll be able to do it!'

★　★　★

The harvesting had to be begun and ended in a single day, and at least six people were needed to cut off the bunches of grapes, rapidly stripping the rows of vines along the hillside. The Bastíus set out before the sun had made up its mind whether to shine or not, and the daughters of Anna Teresa Listru went with them, since the wine would later be shared. As the widow Listru liked to tell her neighbours, she had to re-enact the miracle in Cana: 'Jesus Christ made wine out of water, and I make bread out of wine'.

Maria looked forward all summer to being called in to help, because she loved competing with Andría. No-one ever knew exactly when the harvest would begin, because it was up to old blind Chicchinu Bastíu to decide: exactly one day before it could be smelt in the air that the grapes were about to turn to must. His grandchildren would carry him out to the vineyard every day, and he would close his eyes and solemnly sniff the sea wind as it lightly touched the vines. As the air moved the leaves and rummaged among the tightly clustered grapes, the old man, like an expert midwife, was certain he could detect the voice of the wine before it was born. Maria never tired of hearing the story.

'They say he can tell the exact day!' she had said to Tzia Bonaria, in an attempt to astonish her with this mysterious power of divination. The old woman listened with a half-smile, not particularly impressed.

'Well . . . it's no surprise if Chicchinu Bastíu and the wine understand each other. His nose is never out of his glass, so he's bound to know the smell.'

The little girl's eyes grew wider as suspicion gnawed away at her belief in this marvel.

'Are you saying he's a cheat then?'

'Are there any grapes still left in the vineyard the next day?'

'No, we always pick them all before sunset.'

'Then he can't be a cheat.' Tzia Bonaria, making no attempt to keep a straight face, lowered her eyes to her sewing again. She knew how much Maria enjoyed harvesting the grapes with the Bastíu family; it was one of the few times she allowed her to miss school.

★ ★ ★

While Andría was busy emptying their pail, Maria tried to solve the mystery of the vineyard air. She lowered a fat bunch of grapes into the basin of water at the end of the row and lifted it out again twice as heavy. Then she buried her face among the grapes, sniffing furiously in her search for the hidden clue. One grape had fermented and rotted in the sun, but once she had taken that out there was nothing left but the normal smell of ripe grapes, much more like a colour than a smell. Disappointed, she consoled herself by biting into a lukewarm grape as she absent-mindedly watched the heads of the others emerge one by one from the rows of vines.

The noise seemed to be coming from behind her, near the low wall. At first it was no more than a whimper, a stifled protest, then it became more definite. Maria moved towards the place it seemed to be coming from, flattening the dry grass with her rapid steps. It was as if the little wall itself was weeping. Maria followed its irregular line for several metres without finding anything to dispel that impression. The faint sound was coming straight from the stones at the top.

'Maria, I'm back!' Andría said impatiently from the row of vines, but the girl took no notice, continuing to move cautiously along the boundary wall.

'Wait, I'm looking at something.'

She stopped at the exact spot the sound seemed to be coming from and stared at the low wall in silence. The sun had already tired of the vines and was sinking rapidly, throwing giant distorted shadows across the ground. Andría's ungainly shadow appeared beside her own.

'What are you doing? The others have nearly finished.'

She put her finger to her lips to keep him quiet and pointed at the wall.

'Listen.'

The wailing was unmistakable, lighter now and struggling somewhat, but distinct enough to create astonishment on the boy's childish face. A minute or two later the Listru sisters and the whole Bastíu family were listening at the wall, forgetting that the whole vineyard must be stripped before sunset. Bonacatta held back a little, shuddering at each wail from the black stones, while Regina and

Giulia looked on in silence, with anxious glances at Salvatore Bastíu and his wife, who were arguing in confusion as they stared at the wall.

'A penitent soul,' said Giannina Bastíu, piously crossing herself. '*Requiemeternamdonaeisdomine . . .*'

In response a loud sob came from the wall. Salvatore shook his head, unconvinced.

'No, this is no Christian. It has to be a devil! We must call Don Frantziscu to bless the vineyard first thing tomorrow, or a whole year's vintage will have to be thrown away.'

Nicola Bastíu seemed little interested in his parents' teleological debate. Rooting about like a wild boar, he examined the base of the dry wall, and explored the cracks between the stone blocks with dirty fingers and knitted brow. Then he climbed over the boundary to look at it from Manuele Porresu's land on the other side. After a minute or two he stood up with an air of abrupt finality and gave his father a strange look.

'They've moved the boundary.'

Salvatore Bastíu held his son's eyes just long enough to believe him, before the wall groaned again and there was no need for anything more to be said.

'The damn sons of bitches, so that's what the wailing was!'

Husband and wife and Nicola, all seized by the same fear, began tearing away stones from the top of the low wall, sending them tumbling between their feet on both sides of the boundary. They seemed in the grip of some furious anxiety which infected the others, who also started demolishing the wall.

They found the small jute sack in the middle, carefully placed between two concave stones that had been crudely hollowed out with the obvious purpose of making room for it. Nicola pulled out his pocket-knife under the tense gaze of his parents. The blade made a dry sound as it sliced through the dirty cloth, to reveal something feebly struggling inside the little bag.

It was a puppy.

When they saw what had been buried in the bag they all made the sign of the cross. Even Nicola.

★ ★ ★

Salvatore Bastíu had never believed night was a time for serious thought. Night was night and that was all there was to it. Any sensible person knew you must look for good advice during your waking hours, because every new dawn is an ambush from which you must protect yourself in any way you can. To be on the safe side, he never left home without first sharpening his pocket-knife and had brought up his children to keep their eyes and ears open. Nicola had needed to learn about life more hurriedly than Andría, because he was not a boy who had come into the world to stand still. This was why his father did not wait until dark to take him along to the house of Bonaria Urrai together with everything they had found in the wall, including the dog.

Sitting at the Urrai kitchen table, father and son watched in silence as Tzia Bonaria's thin fingers conducted an examination, while Maria sat by the fire with the puppy asleep on her knees.

'This was meant to be nasty,' Tzia Bonaria said, carefully fingering the strange collection of objects found in the sack with the little animal.

Salvatore Bastíu was getting impatient.

'Yes, of course it's not good news. But how does this affect the boundary?'

Tzia Bonaria lifted up a little cord thick with knots, its ends interwoven like a necklace round a piece of sun-reddened basalt the size of a nut.

'It ties it in place, keeps it fixed.'

'But they've moved it by at least a metre! And how the hell can they have managed to do that . . . it can't be more than three days since I was last on the farm.'

'Three days can be more than enough if there are others to help. Anyway, the intention was to move the boundary once and for all. And that no-one should even notice.'

'Well, but I noticed . . . ' Nicola said with a half-smile.

Bonaria had a soft spot for the eldest Bastíu boy, but that did not prevent her from giving him a sharp look.

'Don't try to be smarter than you are, Coleddu. You only noticed because the dog survived. If he had died, you can be sure the old boundary line would have died with him.'

The old woman went on fingering the tightly tied nut of basalt while her eyes moved from the objects to her visitors. It was as if she were waiting for something. Salvatore Bastíu suddenly came to a decision:

'Porresu will pay for this.'

'You can't be sure it was him that was responsible.'

'What clearer proof can you want?' Salvatore said angrily, pointing at the objects but being careful not to touch them. 'This is what they've done, they've cast a spell on me to steal themselves a metre of land!'

Bonaria Urrai shook her head gently and said nothing more, but her thin fingers went on playing with the stone.

Forgotten beside the fire until that moment, Maria said:

'I'll call the dog Mosè!'

Nicola, Salvatore and Bonaria turned to her in surprise.

'It's not his fault, I want to keep him.'

Seeing the eager light in the girl's face, the old woman smiled despite herself.

'So you can, as long as you look after him yourself.'

Maria nodded, accepting a permission she had never actually asked for. A dog intended to die as a curse needed no excuse me or thank you. She continued to sit by the fire nursing the puppy, while the Bastíus were ushered to the door in a silence heavy with plans. When Bonaria returned and the two were alone, she went to sit with Maria by the fire. Silently moving her lips as if chewing, she threw the round stone, the cord and the bag one by one into the flames. What could burn, did, and the rest was lost in the ashes, its significance fading.

'I wanted to burn those things too, Tzia. Fire purifies everything.'

Maria spoke softly, stroking the dog as she watched. The old woman raised her eyes to look at her, then stood up with an air of firm finality.

'Come on, it's late: Christians inside and

animals outside. Put him out, then go to bed, because tomorrow it's school for you.'

Bonaria shook out her apron while Mosè distrustfully watched Maria open the door to the yard. Soon the little girl was asleep, but the old woman went on sitting before the fire in thought, her eyes fixed on the gradually dying embers. The round stone lay like a still heart in the midst of the ashes, its porous surface blackened by the fire, but far from purified.

5

The only thing that Bonacatta, Anna Teresa Listru's eldest daughter, had in common with her sister Maria was her black eyes. Strong as an ox, she had worked for eight years as a servant in the house of Giuanni Asteri to save up for her trousseau, and now, even though she was wearing the most fashionable skirt in her wardrobe, she was sitting in the living room with no more grace than a ruined *nuraghe*.

Members of both the engaged couple's families were sitting on the edges of their chairs and raising their voices, as they tentatively sipped malmsey wine and laughed loudly at things that in normal circumstances they would hardly dignify with a smile. Skirts rustled along the invisible boundary between the two families; the sisters and cousins of the bride-to-be were serving *amaretti* and forti-fied wine with the falsely timid smiles and lowered gazes of well-brought-up folk. Only Maria's curiosity kept her eyes level with her tray as she could not resist weighing up her future in-laws. They were not rich, no, because no seriously rich man would ever marry the daughter of a widow with no property. But neither were they poor, judging by the ritual gifts they had brought for the bride-to-be: a medal of Our Lady of the Assumption on a gold chain, an antique ring and a large ugly pin for the headscarves that Bonacatta never wore, drawn as she was to the new fashion from the continent. Maria was sure that not even all this gold worn together would ever be enough to make Bonacatta beautiful, but in the end that was not the point. The gifts were a sort of votive offering to the supine figure of the Madonna of the Assumption, not so much ornaments as items for barter: coral in exchange for favours, gold to balance against devotion. If Bonacatta had ever reflected on the matter, she would have realized that in reality there was no devotion whatever behind all this display-cabinet ostentation, but reflection had never been a strong point with Sisinnio Listru's eldest daughter.

Her betrothed, Antonio Luigi Cau, was sitting in obvious discomfort beside his mother, as motionless as a stuffed animal. He seemed tall even when sitting down and so far had said nothing at all, leaving his parents to do the talking, partly because that was the custom and partly because there was little he could say that had not already been said.

'Is this girl another of your daughters, Anna? I thought you only had three.' The bridegroom's mother's eyes examined Maria's slender figure, while her fat fingers removed two *amaretti* from her tray.

'My youngest, our Mariedda. I gave her away as a *fill'e anima* seven years ago, but when we need help she's happy to come and give a hand.'

Anna Teresa Listru spoke in a self-satisfied voice, elaborating the truth to her own advantage as was her habit. This unexpected loquacity gave her daughter's future mother-in-law a chance to address Maria directly.

'And whose soul-child are you, my dear?'

For a moment the hubbub of conversation dropped to a whisper as Maria answered, unaware of the flash of alarm in her mother's eyes.

'I was taken by Tzia Bonaria Urrai, the seamstress, who had no children of her own.'

The silence that greeted this statement lasted long enough to reveal embarrassment, before the fiancé's mother gave a short smile and removed another *amaretto* from the tray.

'An excellent person, Bonaria, we know her. I believe she even made a suit for Vincenzo when he was president of the committee — you remember, Bissè?' She winked at her husband who was listening with interest. 'Her hands

49

are worth their weight in gold, though of course she doesn't really need the work. She will certainly treat you well,' she said to Maria, with a sideways glance at Anna Teresa Listru.

'She treats me as her own daughter, I lack for nothing.' Maria's response was as automatic as it was polite, a perfect answer already used a thousand times. 'Do please take another *amaretto*, Bonacatta made them.'

Maria proffered her tray like a beggar anxious for alms, with a curious hint of a bow that served for a moment to conceal her expression from those round her. Everyone else seemed struck dumb as if by witchcraft, so much so that her eldest sister took the opportunity to break the silence with a trivial remark.

'Maria's lucky, what a great privilege to have two families. And from now on I'll have two as well, won't I? Because you two will be another mother and father to me as though I was your own daughter.'

Miraculously, her smile made the bride-to-be even uglier, as it disclosed an extensive array of powerful teeth. But her comment did succeed in damping down the embarrassment and bringing out a few forced smiles.

'It won't do you much good, Bonacatta, because I was never one to mollycoddle my children! Ask Antonio Luigi if I was ever a loving father, just ask him!' Vincenzo Cau gave a hoarse laugh, stiff in his starched, cream-coloured formal suit that had probably fitted him nicely five years before.

His comment reminded everyone sharply of the purpose of the meeting, but while everyone else laughed with relief, his wife confined herself to an ambiguous smile and darted one more sharp glance at the little girl still fearlessly circulating with her tray. Antonio Luigi reached out a calloused hand for the *amaretti*, while Maria raised her eyes to meet the gaze of the man who was to marry her sister.

'Do you know how to make sweets?'

It was the first time all afternoon that Maria had heard him speak; he had a deep clear solemn baritone. A farmer working his own land, Antonio Luigi Cau at twenty-five had already been an adult for at least ten years.

Surprised by the direct question, the girl lowered her eyes to her tray. 'I can make fruit shapes from almond paste. Pears, apples, strawberries . . . animals too!'

'Clever girl, because that's important too; it isn't only with their mouths that people eat.'

The sunburnt fingers of her future brother-in-law grabbed an *amaretto*, lightly

51

scraping its base on the tray. Maria took a step back as if she had herself been touched, pulling the tray to herself and looking up at him again. Unaware of her reaction, Antonio Luigi Cau had already lost interest in her, chewing the *amaretto* with closed lips as he turned away to listen to what other people were saying. Maria stood near him for a few seconds more, then her future aunt stole another almond sweetmeat from the tray, forcing her to move on. During the rest of the engagement party Maria stayed silent and helpful, avoiding everyone's eye when she got up to help clear away the dishes.

She saw Tzia Bonaria again at nightfall, when she brought home a basketful of left-over *amaretti* as well as a raging fever she could hardly admit to.

'How did it go?'

'Decent people, as far as I could see.'

'And is he a decent type?'

'Seems to be.' Then she said quietly, with a thin smile: 'He's tall.'

Bonaria laughed, carefully folding away her last piece of cloth for the day, some wool she had cut into the shape of a little coat.

'Well, that's fine then. But don't you think it might be useful to be able to do something more than just pick figs from a tree without needing a ladder?'

Maria laughed in her turn, but felt herself blush with embarrassment. If Bonaria noticed, she showed no sign of it.

'They've fixed on the thirteenth of May, so it won't be too close to Whitsun.'

'Will they need you to help?'

'Yes, they've asked me for the pastries and the bread.'

'As far as the pastries are concerned, fine. But for the bread only if it's a Saturday. I don't want you missing school.'

Maria had never been eager to go and work in her old home before, but now she dug in her heels like a deaf mule.

'I've hardly ever missed school, and the place won't fall down if I have a day off because my sister's getting married!'

Bonaria gave way only after repeated insistence, and as she did so she felt there was some important detail she did not know about. The lack of enthusiasm for visiting her mother's home that Maria had shown from the first had always deeply reassured Bonaria, even though she could not honestly have sworn that she had never made any attempt to encourage this indifference. Until the day she had first met Maria and her mother in the shop, Bonaria had considered herself as suffering from a perfect anguish, unique in that it could never be assuaged. She knew the world she was taking the girl from; in fact she knew it so well she had never felt any need to be aware of its every form. So she had not been surprised that Maria had never shown any obvious homesickness since deep down, in the privacy of her solitary infancy, the girl must always have known that her destiny did not lie in her old home. But now, faced with Maria's insistence on helping with the preparations for Bonacatta's wedding, the confidence of Bonaria Urrai wavered. She had no women friends or sisters she could have talked to about what was worrying her, but even if there had been any, she would have kept her worries to herself.

★ ★ ★

Anna Teresa Listru had spoken the truth to her daughter's future mother-in-law when she claimed that she really did call Maria back to her old home whenever she needed her. But what Anna Teresa had not admitted was that Maria did not always come when she was called. Bonaria Urrai examined the reasons for every request like a hawk, reserving the right to refuse if she considered it unsuitable. Not that she ever said no in so many words. It was enough to insist that the hem of some skirt had to be finished urgently, or that

Doctor Mastinu was coming to perform a vital check-up, and those who were willing to understand understood. Only in exceptional circumstances did the old woman agree to the little girl going out to work in the countryside, most often for gathering in the grapes with the Bastíu family, or for the olive harvest. But the widow Listru took the view that Maria believed she had been transformed into a princess ever since she first went to live with the Urrai woman, because she never lifted a single potato from the soil or bent down to dig for a beetroot, or immersed herself in the rice-fields to be paid for piecework like her sisters; and above all, she had made it clear that she could never be called out to bake bread at four in the morning. Anna Teresa Listru never complained openly about this, but she did still feel that Maria's privileged position should bring some extra advantage for herself, over and above the fact that one hungry mouth had been removed from the family round her table. What particularly annoyed her was the apparent obsession on the part of the elderly Urrai woman that Maria must go to school regularly. Anna Teresa Listru found this hard to understand. After all, the little girl had reached Middle School Grade Three, and had already learned more there than she would ever need in life. There was no reason why Maria should not begin to repay a little of what she had been given, remembering whose saucepan had had to fill her stomach until the age of six. So Bonacatta's wedding had seemed to the widow Listru an ideal occasion to put a little pressure on Bonaria Urrai to allow Maria to miss a day or two of school to help with the enormous quantity of cakes and bread that would have to be baked for the occasion.

Yet despite the widow Listru's worst fears, the old Urrai woman seemed to make no difficulties, since Maria turned up on the afternoon set for making the almond confectionery without having to be asked for twice. Perhaps Anna Teresa would be able to make the most of this after all, taking advantage of the fact that the great central table in the living-room had become the frenetic scene of these unprecedented events.

The ingredients necessary for the *amaretti* made a fine display, and a fragrant chain was formed in which every available pair of hands, including those of the bride-to-be, had its own precise moment for action. On one side, stored in a large glazed earthenware basin, were sweet almonds chopped into tiny fragments, ready to be mixed with flour and egg to produce a biscuit to be baked in the oven with an almond or half a candied cherry stuck in the middle. Anna Teresa had advised using plenty of flour and being economical with the almonds, even if this would make the sweetmeats very soft. Meanwhile, the other side of the long table was dominated by a small mountain of almonds cut into thin strips waiting to be crystallized in sugar with grated lemon peel: once cold and cut into diamonds, this would become a form of country toffee which only the strongest teeth would be able to get through. Maria's job, while her mother and sisters chattered, was grating the lemon peel. Anna Teresa Listru wasted no time in getting to the point.

'Are you pleased you didn't have to go to school today?'

'Well . . . I never mind school, but today's a special day.'

Regina and Giulia exchanged looks, while Bonacatta worked eggs into the dough to soften it. Giulia said, 'I don't know how you don't get bored always sitting there, I hated every day when I had to be at school.'

'And school got its own back and serve you right: you ended up having to do Fourth Grade twice!' Bonacatta said maliciously, strong in the authority of her twenty-five years.

'You're the one who did the most studying,

you are!' Regina had never admitted that she had really rather liked school, and Bonacatta never missed a chance to add to her sister's embarrassment.

Giulia's humiliation found unexpected relief from her mother, who usually never intervened in such squabbles for fear they might degenerate into trouble for herself.

'There's no point in school,' Anna Teresa said firmly. 'Once you've learned how to sign your name and count change in the shop, that's enough, it's not as if you're going to be a doctor. I only reached Third Grade in Elementary School, and no-one ever criticized me for that, not even the bookworms!'

This was something Anna Teresa Listru loved saying, because she believed it was important not to encourage her daughters to aim too high. Giulia in particular had lived all her nineteen years with this object in mind, as her mother never failed to point out to the neighbours. 'She's like me when I was a girl, lots of common sense and no fancy ideas,' she would state, affectionately patting the shoulder of the girl who was now once more her youngest daughter.

'But Maria enjoys school,' Anna Teresa continued, determined to pursue the subject further. 'What is it you want to be, Maria, a doctor of almonds? Or a professor of hems and buttonholes like Tzia Bonaria Urrai?'

The others laughed, but Maria refused to be intimidated; it was by no means the first time her mother had teased her in this way, so she had known what to expect from the very first.

'School can be useful for all kinds of things, even for making cakes.'

'Of course. Before we went to school we had no idea how to make cakes, that's true. But what on earth are you getting at?'

Maria stopped grating the lemon she was holding and picked up one of the balls of almond paste that Regina had just finished shaping. Then she held it out to her mother with a defiant expression.

'Do you know why *gueffus* are called *gueffus*?'

Anna Teresa Listru stared at her as though she had gone mad, while her sisters stopped work to enjoy the scene.

'What a silly question! That's what they're called because they've always been called that.'

'Yes, but why? Why aren't they called bowler hats, for example, or . . . backgammon?'

Bonacatta was unable to suppress a laugh, immediately provoking a furious glare from her mother.

'I don't know. Do you? If you do, be so

59

good as to instruct us, Maestra Maria. Please explain this fundamental fact for us.'

'Because the word refers to the Guelphs, the soldiers who backed the Pope against the Emperor in the Middle Ages.'

'How interesting. Did they fire cannonballs made of almond paste?'

This time they all laughed, but Maria went on regardless.

'They got this name because, when we put them into paper cups, we cut the edges of the paper with square teeth like the battlements on the Guelph castles.'

Anna Teresa Listru had listened to the beginning of this explanation with a mixture of irritation and amusement, but now she was just amused.

'You can't really believe such nonsense . . . '

With a gesture of exaggerated elegance she picked up one of the *gueffus* from the flour-covered table and raised it to her mouth, biting it in half. She closed her eyes as she chewed, then suddenly opened them wide, as if astonished.

'May I be struck by lightning! Now I know how it got its name, it even tastes different! If you hadn't told me, Maria, I'm sure I'd never have known what I was missing!'

Giulia and Regina who, torn between

believing and disbelieving, had each furtively bitten into one of the *gueffus* just to enjoy the taste, nearly choked with laughter while Bonacatta, anxious not to disturb the preparation of her cakes, merely smiled at Maria's disappointment:

'That's enough teaching for one day. Now we have work to do: finish the lemons for me, because I have to ice the *pirichittus*. And I warn you that if you ask me why they have this name, I know the reason why.'

'She'll tell you when you grow up.' Regina got a box on the ear for this impertinence, while Maria went back to grating lemon peel with a passion worthy of a greater cause.

For three whole days the bride's home became an ants' nest of relatives and neighbours coming and going with baskets full of fresh ingredients and borrowed trays on which the finished cakes were laid. The Listru sisters worked almost without a break, alternating tasks to bring miraculously to life an army of *capigliette* decorated with sugar lace, kilos of *tiliccas* swollen with *saba*, baskets full of *aranzadas* with their spicy aroma, tin boxes full of crisp little sugar dolls, and hundreds of round almond *gueffus*, individually wrapped like sweets in white tissue paper with its edges fringed like the battlements of the Guelph towers. There was not a room in the house with space in it for anything more, and Giulia and Regina had to move basketfuls of finished delicacies off their beds before they could fall asleep in the gentle fragrance of orange-flower water.

Each evening Maria went home to the house of Bonaria Urrai, and before falling asleep would enjoy innocent day-dreams about the tall man her sister was going to marry.

6

On the day of Bonacatta's wedding two
terrible things happened besides the wedding
itself. First, Maria did something she had
promised not to do. While everyone else was
busy dressing the bride and doing her hair,
she went into her mother's bedroom. The
shutters were closed but, even in the
semi-darkness, she could make out the shapes
under the white cloths spread over the
baskets on the bed that contained the bread
freshly baked that morning. The two-tone
Formica wardrobe covered a whole wall, and
the oval mirror on the door in the middle of it
glared out at the whole room like the eye of a
Cyclops. Maria knew she had very little time.
Carefully she lifted the white cloths one by
one and searched the bread-baskets until she
found what she was looking for, a hamper
arranged right under the mirror.

Perfectly circular and decorated with little
doves and flowers, her sister's nuptial loaf
seemed finer and more beautiful than when
she had last seen it on the baking shovel: a
filigree of flour and water, the achievement of
an artistry granted to few women. Maria had

not been allowed to help her mother and Bonacatta prepare it, and even the simple act of looking at it in secret was a violation with possible consequences that filled her blood with a rush of heat, spiced by the good strong smell with which the room was pregnant. She had no ulterior motive in wanting to look at the loaf, beyond the desire with which those who visit an exhibition of famous pictures buy the ticket which confirms the fact that they will never be able to own them. But as she bent to take a closer look at the bread her eyes fell on the mirror, which showed her not only the bread but also herself.

She could hear the subdued chatter of those dressing the bride deep within the house, but to Maria the scent of the bread was far more powerful than any sound. Sinfully imagining herself in the eyes of another woman's man, she stood up and studied herself without understanding. The bride of the day was not Bonacatta but the self she saw in the mirror, because in that mysterious world of reflections the bride-groom's gaze had fallen on her face like a hand grasping a fragrant *amaretto*. But the little girl in the mirror was not yet ready to be a bride: her immature breasts pressed so weakly against the shirt with its faded flowers that not even the thin material could make anything of them. Impulsively, she unbuttoned her shirt in a feverish search for a fuller femininity; but all she could see was the soft and still childish quality of her skin, and the little baptismal chain shining against it as incongruously as a golden wound. She followed the tentative curve of her naked breast to its tiny extremity then stopped, disappointed that nothing more ample was visible. Her disappointment blinded her to her slender but genuine grace; all she could see through the transparent skin over her ribs was a feeble approximation at being female.

It was to remedy this discourtesy on the part of time that she turned back to the basket at her feet, her attention drawn once more to the special bread for the bridal couple; she was aware that this bread ring was even more important than the rings for their fingers, destined though it was first for the offertory and then for an eternity behind glass, hung on the wall after being sprayed with wood-polish against woodworm and mould. Fully aware of its importance she lifted it with great care and lowered it slowly on to her head, where it fitted as closely as if specially made for her. In the mirror she was beautiful at last, a bread queen celebrated in the forbidden smell of a silent coronation. But even as she smiled, the sound of footsteps in the corridor made her turn in alarm. Or perhaps she was frightened by the inappropriate weight of that malevolent bread, an ornament for a day that was not her own.

Unfortunately her first thought was for her naked breast. As she clumsily tried to ward off approaching danger by searching for the edges of her open shirt, she lurched forward and felt the crown beginning to slip from her head. Her fingers were too slow to save her from disaster, and the bread that was intended to bring good fortune hit the floor with a crisp snap like a breaking of bones. Even so, if this had been all that was lost on the day of Bonacatta's wedding, it would not have been too serious.

What Anna Teresa Listru saw when she opened the door to collect the baskets of bread was nothing but her youngest daughter standing bare-breasted before the wardrobe mirror. And what the bridegroom's mother saw as she came to help was only the *fill'e anima* of Bonaria Urrai standing alone among the covered bread-baskets like an ancient menhir on the June hills. And all that Bonacatta saw, coming up behind them dressed in white, was her nuptial bread in pieces spread over the wine-red tiles of her mother's bedroom floor. None of the women involved in this disaster of reflections was

66

fully aware of Maria, and in that collective blindness lay her only consolation, the only form of intimacy open to her within the walls of that house. As things turned out, the wedding went ahead just the same with very little sense of any bad omens; while Bonacatta wept in desperation, the bread was temporarily stuck back together with white of egg and put into the warm oven for a few minutes, just long enough for it to play its part in the offertory during the wedding service. Maria was declared to have suffered a sudden indisposition which prevented her from being present in the church and, apart from the younger son of the Bastíu family, the only people who might have had any reason to regret her absence knew how things were and kept quiet. When she got home it was already more than an hour after dark, but Bonaria Urrai was not there.

★   ★   ★

The journey in the motorcycle sidecar, an ancient model from just after the war that had stubbornly survived on the potholed roads of the Soreni countryside, was short and extremely bumpy. The *accabadora* was in the passenger seat, and the man who had come to fetch her from her house made no

67

effort whatever at any sort of conversation. When they reached the farm deep in the countryside, the old woman got out quickly. Two dogs had already announced their arrival by barking furiously, and the young woman in a dark coat at the door had clearly already been waiting for them for several minutes. The damaged plaster on the corner of the facade most exposed to the *mistral* revealed indistinctly the rough outlines of bricks made from raw clay, while the moon shining from a clear sky made it possible to discern on the threshing-floor a small brick building with an asbestos roof, probably a henhouse. The windows of the main house were shuttered, giving the impression that it was uninhabited. But this was not the case.

'Thank you for coming,' the woman said, conventionally polite.

The *accabadora* merely nodded and pulled her shawl more tightly round herself, unwilling to stay longer than strictly necessary. They went into the house, leaving the dogs outside to guard the motorcycle. Inside six people were waiting, a whole family assembled round a bare table; at her entry they rose to their feet as if in answer to a roll-call. In addition to the man who had brought her, the husband of the woman who had opened the door, two other men of between thirty and forty inclined their heads as a sign of respect; near the fireplace there were also two little girls in pyjamas, with the sleepy eyes of children who would normally have long been asleep at that hour. The younger was holding a ragdoll dog that must have once been white. Quickly deciding who was in charge, the *accabadora* spoke.

'Where is he?'

The woman indicated with her eyes a wooden door at one side of the room, half hidden by an ancient dresser.

'In there, we only ever move him for his sores now.'

The woman set off, followed in silence by the others in procession.

The only lighting in the bedroom was the lamp on the bedside table, which cast shapeless shadows on the skeletal head of the old man lying under the covers with his head supported by two pillows. He seemed to be asleep.

'How long has he been like this?' the *accabadora* said, approaching the bed while the others spontaneously arranged themselves round them.

'Eight months next week. But two years in all, including the time when we could still have him sitting up.'

The woman was the only one who spoke,

occasionally exchanging a glance with her husband and brothers. The *accabadora* fixed her with her dark eyes.

'Has he asked for me?'

The other shook her head several times, avoiding her gaze as if on the brink of tears.

'No, he hasn't spoken for weeks.' Then she said, 'But I do understand my father.'

Apparently satisfied with this answer, the *accabadora* reached out from her black shawl and lightly touched the old man's bony forehead. At her touch he opened his eyes, silently fixing her with his faded pupils.

'Have you removed his benedictions?'

'All of them. We've also checked the pillows and the mattress. We've even taken off his baptismal medal. There's nothing left to hold him here.' There was something feverish about the woman's voice as she listed the objects. 'And we've put the yoke on him too.'

She went to the bed and slipped her hand under the pillow, taking out a small piece of soft wood roughly carved in the shape of a yoke for oxen. The *accabadora* examined this, then looked again at the elderly figure lying on the bed. When she spoke again it was to issue a peremptory command.

'Leave the room, all of you.'

None of the men showed any inclination to disobey her. But the woman of the house made no sign of moving, so the old woman stared at her. Reluctantly, the woman too left the bedroom, quietly closing the door behind her.

Alone with the old man, the *accabadora* examined him. The wide-open eyes of Tziu Jusepi Vargiu had the irreversible immobility of broken things. Bonaria took hold of his skinny hand, carefully feeling his wrist and forearm, and something in this contact made her wince. The old man gave a hoarse cry.

'So they've called you at last . . . '

With a skeletal grip he drew the hand of the *accabadora* closer, forcing the tall dark figure to bend over him. Weak though he was, the old man's whisper was not lost in the folds of her shawl, and Bonaria Urrai could hear him perfectly. Outside, the family were saying prayers as they waited, but it did not even take the *accabadora* the time she would have needed for a *Pater ave gloria* before she was out of the old man's room, deliberately leaving the door open behind her. The family rose to their feet again. But when Bonaria Urrai turned to the woman and her husband, they must have been sorry they had not been born deaf.

'Antonia Vargiu, for calling me out for no good reason, I curse all present.'

She had never before in all those years

been forced to speak these words but, now that she needed them, they came to her as naturally as her breath.

'For having lied to me by telling me he could not speak, may all your children be cursed, those you already have and those yet unborn.'

'No!' the woman cried out, trying to interrupt her, while the others drew back, muttering exorcisms in subdued voices. 'He was dying . . . even the doctor said so!'

The *accabadora* did not moderate her expression or her tone.

'You know perfectly well your father is not dying, and isn't even near to death. You would do better to give him something to eat. If he dies of hunger, may you never sleep again.'

The little girl with the ragdoll dog burst into tears, but none of the grown-ups tried to comfort her. The *accabadora* left the house without another word. When, less than an hour later, the motorcycle stopped again in front of her home, Maria was still awake and in utter despair.

'Where were you? I was so worried!'

'I was out.'

'Even I knew that, Tzia. Who was that man?'

'No-one you know, Maria. And you

shouldn't be awake at this hour either, it's Monday tomorrow.'

The girl was suddenly angry, and made no effort to hide her anger from the old woman.

'What do I care about school? Where were you?'

Bonaria Urrai, still covered with dust from her journey over the potholes, could not hide her disbelief at this tone of voice.

'I'm not obliged to account to you for where I go, Maria Listru. Or have you become the adult, and am I now the child?'

This sharp riposte was not quite enough to put the girl in her place. She burst out once more:

'I may be little, but surely I have a right to know what's what at home? It's after midnight, and I haven't eaten because I was waiting for you.'

'Oh, so now the worm has turned. Did your sister's wedding fill your stomach too full for you to feed yourself?'

Maria made no reply, but just stared at the face of the old seamstress with her black shawl still wrapped round her as if to shield her from the non-existent cold of the warm May night. Bonaria Urrai realized Maria's silence was full of unsaid things and stared at her in her turn. She slipped off the shawl.

'Tell me what happened,' she said.

That night no one slept: not the Listrus who had good reason to celebrate, nor the Vargius whose reason for celebrating had been snatched from them, nor the two women in the house of Taniei Urrai, sitting with their arms round each other in front of the fireplace as they talked until dawn about a broken loaf of bread and a broken love. It was only when it was already morning and Maria was getting into bed that she remembered that other time Bonaria had gone out at night, five years before when Giacomo Littorra died. She seemed to be thinking in a dreamy underwater confusion of childhood memories, until finally she fell asleep exhausted. But one good thing did come out of all this: she never again needed to invent an excuse for not going to help her mother to bake bread.

7

Four years had passed since the business of the Pran'e boe boundary, and still Nicola Bastíu could not understand how his father had been able to leave the question unresolved as if nothing was amiss. Slashing angrily with his billhook, he was pruning the hedge on the south side of the farm, the side where the olives were, and now and then throwing glances in the opposite direction, over the dry wall to where Manuele Porresu spent days waiting under the pergola of his farm for the right moment to harvest the produce of his fields, now larger by nearly two hundred metres thanks to the altered boundary on the Bastíu side. The others who bordered the area had already completed their harvest, some sooner than others, leaving the air thick with smoke from burnt stubble, which had raised the temperature by a couple of degrees, hardly ideal at that time of year. Nicola scarcely even glanced in their direction before setting himself mercilessly to prune the hedge, with his brother at his side struggling unsuccessfully to keep up with his furious pace.

'Nicò, stop, it makes me feel ill when you go about it like a gorilla.'

'Leave me alone, Andría. Every time I come here and see what that wretch is up to . . .'

Andría knew his brother's repertoire of protests by heart. Nicola would eventually inherit the diminished area when the land was divided, and the thought of having to submit to injustice regarding his future property with no chance of redress redoubled his fury.

'At first it seemed *babbo* wanted to make him pay for it, but then nothing was done, and that man will benefit this year by at least an extra forty thousand kilos before our very eyes!'

Every time he worked along the disputed boundary, Nicola measured with his eye the section he believed to be missing, and estimated the extent of his loss from what Porresu had planted that year. Sometimes it was tomatoes, sometimes melons. This year it was grain.

'*Babbo* has explained to you why.'

'What do I care about *babbo*'s friends, about who knows *babbo*, and about who *babbo*'s afraid of offending! The land's mine, and Porresu's already had his own way once. What is there to stop him moving the boundary again tonight if he wants to, since he's found it's defended by idiots who just stand and watch?'

'He thinks the spell with the dog is still at work in the wall so he won't touch it again, even you know that.'

This was an irrefutable argument, but Nicola was not satisfied: even if it did guarantee the future, it could not restore his lost land. The billhook whistled through the air like a hornet, while brambles fell around them in calculated disorder.

'All I understand is that it's down to me to defend my own property. *Babbo*'s old, he hasn't the will to fight all these people. But to me it matters like hell not to be taken for a ride.'

'But what can you do, Nicola? Are you planning to move the wall and put it back over the grain? Then you too would become guilty of moving other people's boundaries.'

Nicola stopped swinging the billhook and looked at him.

'Even if you can't have back what has been taken from you, at least you can stop the thief from profiting from it.'

'I don't know what you mean.' Andría looked at the sweaty and dusty figure of his brother.

'I know very well what I mean. If Porresu's

sons are dreaming of qualifying as doctors on my money.'

'I wouldn't do anything differently from *babbo*, Nicò. Or you'll end up losing more than you hope to gain.'

'Is it your land, Andría?'

'No, but . . . '

'Then mind your own business, I don't need you telling me how to live.' Then he said with deliberate malice, 'By the way, have you told Maria Urrai yet that you've fallen in love with her, or shall I have to write it up on the wall of her house?'

Andría's silence was heavier than an oath, and it was with this weight between them that they finished clearing the hedge and made a huge pile of the brambles so they could dry out in the sun before being burnt a few days later.

Andría spent the whole afternoon turning over Nicola's words in his mind, unsure whether to believe him really capable of doing what he had threatened. Too discreet to tell his mother, he was, despite his brother's opinion, sufficiently wide awake to understand that it would not be a good idea to discuss the matter with his father or with his friends at the bar. He realized not for the first time that Maria was the only person he could speak to openly, as he watched her sitting on the raffia seat of a chair specially made for her, as by the grudging light of an overcast sky she sewed on a pocket with the expertise of a professional seamstress.

'What do you think he might do?'

'Andrí, he's not that stupid, your brother. He talks like that because he's angry, but he has nothing positive to get his teeth into.'

'You haven't seen him, he can't sleep . . . '

The tawny shape of Mosè was curled up by the empty grate, a survivor of witchcraft sleeping placidly to the sound of the voices of the two young people, exploiting the absence of Bonaria to enjoy the few furtive hours allowed by Maria indoors. The animal's uncritical love seemed to Maria the only thing in the world she had never needed to earn. To calm his nerves Andría went over to bend down and bury his face, with its first traces of a beard, in the dog's soft fur.

'I don't believe he'd ever inflict damage to get even for an injury done to him,' Maria said, 'but if you think he would, you should mention it to your father.'

Had Andría been certain he would have acted at once, even at the cost of a couple of kicks up the bum from his brother, who notwithstanding his seventeen years would have been only too happy to administer them; but as he was by no means certain, he decided that even with all that smoke there was not enough evidence of a fire, and so without realizing it, for the last time in his life, he made a mockery of his own better instinct.

★ ★ ★

A man who values the respect of others may perform good acts gratuitously, but bad acts must be performed out of necessity. If Nicola Bastíu had been asked to account for himself at that moment, he would have had no hesitation in attributing what he was about to do to the necessity that would justify it. Even so he decided to act at night, darkness being already in its way a form of mitigation. He had little time for carrying out what he had planned, since his family thought he had gone to see his friends at the bar, while his friends thought he was still at home. The weather was very much on his side that evening: the air was dry, and a warm wind had got up from the south and was lifting the grass with rough gusts and caressing Porresu's ripe grain with the deceitful hand of a shepherd in a slaughterhouse. There was enough moonlight to see by, but knowing this was not necessarily to his advantage, Nicola moved fast, trying to make the most of the darkest shadows cast by the wall and the trees, and with instinctive respect for the nocturnal silences of the countryside. He needed to drag some of the dry brambles he had recently piled up with Andría over the stone wall, relocating them to the southernmost point of Porresu's farm; it was the only way to be sure that once they burst into flames, the wind would carry the fire in the direction that would cause the greatest possible damage. Everything had to be done quickly and with great care, because Nicola wanted no trace of the brambles dragged across the soft earth to make it easy to detect the perpetrator of the act. Porresu must suspect that he had been had, but not be so certain of it as to be able to bring in the law, exactly as in the case of his own action against the Bastíus four years before. With a wind like that, the fire could easily have been started by flames from the field of a neighbour, perhaps one of those whose recently burnt stubble had been smouldering angrily on the blackened earth. It was always possible that the stubble had not burnt out properly. It was possible that the wind had got stronger. It was also possible that someone you had dismissed as a fool was showing you up as a fool in return. Not the likeliest story, but Nicola counted on it as he lit the tinder to set fire to the piled-up brambles.

By the time the flames were rising into the sky like a curse, the eldest son of Salvatore Bastíu was already on the way to his car; now let the wind do its work, he had already finished his own work for the day. The rifle shot that whistled through the night hit him just before he reached the road, leaving him stretched out on the beaten earth, with no explanation or shout of any kind.

8

The commander of the Carabinieri, a Calabrian of Sicilian descent, knew immediately that the story was untrue, but he also knew that with eight witnesses ready to swear that there had been a hunting accident, there was no point in being pedantic. There are places where truth and the opinion of the majority can overlap, and in that mysterious world where people agree to agree, Soreni was a minor capital of morality. The statement was written down, signed and filed, and Nicola was brought home with a severe wound in his leg, but more ashamed of having failed in his intended revenge than of having compelled his father to ask friends to lie to cover this failure.

Fully aware of the cover-up used to explain the incident at Pran'e boe farm to the law, Manuele Porresu went to church on Sunday on his wife's arm walking tall, proud of having created justice out of his own unjust act, and conscious of having won the silent respect even of those who had previously believed him to be in the wrong. On the other hand, what most worried Salvatore Bastíu was that his son should have appeared stupid, so that he himself would have to judge him stupid. No one at Soreni was ever more mocked and marginalized than a stupid person, because if shrewdness, force and intelligence were powerful weapons, stupidity had no greater enemy than itself, its fundamental unpredictability making it even more dangerous in friends than in enemies. The trouble was that in neither case could a reputation for stupidity ever be accompanied by respect, something of enormous importance in a place that, when all was said and done, offered few other advantages.

Giannina Bastíu went shopping with her head held high in spite of everything, but the malicious spark in the eyes of those who asked in sugary tones after Nicola encouraged her to lie and claim that he would soon be fully recovered. In fact his leg deteriorated daily, and despite careful medication, the wound became infected, causing a persistent fever and twice forcing Dr Mastinu to reopen the suture to release pus. Maria and Bonaria had to wait before they could pay a courtesy call, because Nicola refused to see anyone, partly from shame and partly because he did not want his friends to know of his condition. But after two weeks immobile and confined to bed, he had turned into a caged lion who could scarcely even tolerate attention from the doctor and his own family. As the days passed his leg gave no sign of healing, until even Dr Mastinu realized no further improvement could be expected.

Once word spread through the local bars that Nicola's leg would probably have to be amputated, the so-called hunting accident began to seem less amusing.

* * *

It was the first time Bonaria had seen Nicola since the incident at Pran'e boe. Even when the young man began to receive visitors, the elderly seamstress had insisted on taking her time, and had not even sent Maria to ask after him. It was as if she had distanced herself from the event and from the person responsible for it, as if the incident in which Nicola nearly lost his life had in fact killed him and then brought him back to life in some distant foreign country that could not be reached without a very long journey.

The bed where they had put him was the double bed in the guestroom reserved for visiting aunts and uncles staying over for festivals, and otherwise used as a store for valued objects. Nicola sat in the middle of the bed supported by a mass of cushions, wearing a simple light-coloured shirt and with his injured leg outside the covers to facilitate medical attention. The coloured chenille bed-spread featured an indiscreet fantasy of little *putti* carrying abundant cornucopias, but thanks to an irreverent play of super-impositions they also looked as if they were holding up his gangrenous limb, passing it from one to another on their chubby little arms. Above this baroque fresco Nicola lay like an obstinate stain, grim of eye and word.

'They say I can't get better. Even Dr Schintu has been here from Gavoi, and he says nothing can be done. They're going to have to take off my leg.'

He looked accusingly at Bonaria, as if the blame for this judgement was flitting round the room in the air and could not wait to find someone to settle on. In case the gravity of the disaster was not entirely clear, Nicola added:

'I shall die.'

Bonaria Urrai looked at the pale figure lying on the bed and clenched her hands in her lap. Until that moment she had deliberately avoided his censorious gaze, because it is never a good idea to apportion blame on a sickbed. When she spoke, it was in a light clear voice, as if chatting about trivial matters.

'You aren't going to die, they're only going to remove one leg.'

'That's the same thing. Isn't a horse dead when it goes lame? Or do they feed it on cripple fodder?'

'You're not a horse, Nicola.'

'Of course I'm not a horse. That's why I deserve something better than to spend the rest of my life mourning for myself.'

'You wouldn't be the first or the last.'

'I'd rather kill myself.'

Bonaria heard him with steely eyes. Despite her fondness for Nicola, her bony ringless hands showed him no pity, locked together like a ball of wool ready for use. Her voice had become as cold as the surrounding air, as if the old woman had turned herself into a bracing draught to freshen the unhealthy atmosphere in the room.

'The Lord giveth and the Lord taketh away. We can't always have what we want.'

Nicola laughed, a dry laugh, full of the rage of a man who has never before felt powerless.

'Have they turned you into a priest, Tzia Bonaria? We have a woman priest at Soreni and no-one knew it! Who's going to tell Don Frantziscu that the daughter of the Urrai family has become his curate?'

'Poking fun at me won't help you.' Bonaria was not bothered even by what others would have considered an insufferable lack of respect.

Nicola decided to make the most of it, and put all his cards on the table.

'But I can change the circumstances of my death. Or you can . . . '

Bonaria Urrai grew wary, fixing him with eyes like thorns.

'I don't understand,' she said tonelessly.

'Yes you do.' Nicola lowered his voice to a murmur, ruthless in his desperation. 'Santino Littorra has told me what you did when his father died. I'm not asking for anything different.'

Bonaria suddenly sprang out of her chair as if she had been scalded, took several steps towards the window so as to have her back to Nicola, and when she turned round again the expression in her eyes was one he had never seen before.

'You're talking about things that have nothing to do with you, and Santino is wrong to do the same. And whatever he said, the two cases have nothing in common. Giacomo Littorra was dying.'

'And I'm already dead but they can't bury me.' Bonaria made an angry gesture with her hand, more expressive than any word.

'Do you really think my job is to kill people who haven't the courage to face their problems?'

'No, I believe it's to help those who can't bear to suffer any more.'

'That's Our Lord's job, not mine. Doing what is right has never mattered to you, so are you now trying to get me to do what is wrong?'

Nicola, not much inclined to respect divine roles in the comedy in which he himself played the principal part, was suddenly impatient with Bonaria's evasiveness. He called for his mother in a loud voice. She immediately hurried into the room, drying her hands on her apron.

'What is it, Nicò?'

'Tzia Bonaria's turning into a priest, Ma. She's already quoting the scriptures like someone who has to live on alms. Just listen to her!'

Giannina turned to Bonaria in confusion, but the elderly woman had not moved, and held Nicola's feverish gaze with a neutral expression.

'But what are you saying, Nicola? Is that the way to talk to people who come to pay you a visit?'

'Your son's not well and is saying silly things, Giannina. Don't listen, I'm not listening to him either.'

'I'm not saying silly things. But you are, coming here on two legs to tell me I can walk on one leg alone. That's the way of priests, and stupid people.'

'Nicola, you know why I'm telling you things. There's no point in wasting your anger on me.'

'Then why are you talking like a woman who knows nothing about real life?'

'Only one person in this room knows nothing about real life. If you had any sense you'd thank your guardian angel for the miracle that you're still alive. After what happened you could easily have been dead and buried, with the rest of us in mourning round your grave.'

'Spending my whole life in bed, you call that a miracle? Being carried on a chair when I need to shit, you call that a miracle? Certainly I was a miracle once, a man with only one equal in Soreni, and maybe not even that. Now I'm a cripple, not even worth the air I breathe. I'd have been a hundred times better dead!'

Bonaria made no response, turning towards the window from where the light of what was still full day was painting the room an unreal warm rose colour. The little *putti* on the coverlet glistened rudely in this luminous embrace, creating among the folds of chenille the optical illusion of a hysterical infantile dance. Bonaria snatched her shawl from the chair as a prelude to departure. Going out she said:

'If this is what you really believe, Nicola, I think you're wrong. If all it needs to make a man is a leg, then every table is more of a man than you are.'

Giannina Bastíu irritably reproved her silenced son, then ran out after Bonaria. The two women faced each other in silence in the narrow corridor, while the sound of angry little movements, as abrupt as Nicola's condition permitted, came from the bed inside the room. After waiting nervously for a minute or two, Giannina whispered:

'He won't accept it. What can we do?'

'Try getting the priest to come and see him.'

'Don Frantziscu? And what can he do for my son who doesn't even believe in God?'

Bonaria pursed her lips and she looked at her friend.

'I don't know, Giannina, but in a time of weakness some would rather be believers than tough guys. Maybe the priest could convince him in the name of God to accept himself as he is.'

Giannina Bastíu nodded, but with a hint of resignation. Deep down, the idea of her son becoming a believer was no easier to believe than the fact that her son was a cripple.

9

The bicycle was upside down, propped on its saddle and handlebars. Andría Bastíu was turning the back wheel slowly with his hand, while his eyes searched for the thorn that was probably what had punctured the inner tube. Maria came out of the back door with a basin half-full of water, which she set down beside the bicycle.

'Don't worry, if you were on your way to Turrixeddu it's bound to be only a little one. You should dip the tube in the water then you'll be able to see exactly where the air's coming out.'

Andría did not share this view. Showing no sign of having heard her, he ran the tyre through his fingers in search of the telltale object, patient and silent as a miner.

'Andría, I can't stand here all afternoon just for a punctured tyre.'

Maria's voice disturbed his concentration, and he lifted his eyes from the suspended wheel with an interrogative air.

'If you've got things you have to do, go and get on with them. I have to finish this. But I couldn't have done it at home, Nicola is only just back from the hospital. I can't start working on a bike in the yard right under his window.'

Maria nodded, going to sit on the kerb in front of Bonaria Urrai's house, oblivious of the fact that she was wearing new jeans.

'How is he?'

'He makes me sick. Growling like an animal, attacking everybody and saying all the time he wants to die.'

'I can understand him up to a point, but it must be difficult for the rest of you.'

'He was never an easy person, but this is the worst thing that could have happened to him. Mamma cries in secret, but dad pretends everything's fine and that enrages Nicola even more. It seems that everything I do gets on his nerves.'

Meanwhile Andría had taken off the tyre and extracted the inner tube, and begun to pump it up with his little white pump.

'I'd like to go and see him, but I don't want to intrude.'

'It might not be a good idea, but maybe with you he would control himself.'

Andría turned the tube slowly in the basinful of water, until from an invisible point a tell-tale column of little bubbles rose.

'Got you, you little horror! Now let's have the patch, and we'll seal it up,' Andría said

93

with satisfaction. 'The less there is to see, the worse it really is, that's always the way.'

★ ★ ★

Ever since they had cut off his right leg at the hospital at Mont'e Sali, Nicola slept four hours a night, and then only after sedation. Dr Mastinu said this was normal, that it needed a little time. But Giannina Bastíu had her doubts, because Nicola had never been in the habit of making a fuss about pain. He had broken bones no less than seven times. As a small boy he had never been afraid either of heights or depths, with nests up in trees and snakes down in ditches always an irresistible challenge to him, and taking risks had been his favourite game, to the perpetual despair of his mother and a certain ill-concealed satisfaction on the part of his father. Once at football he had even broken a bone in his hand, a tiny little bone that no-one had ever heard of before, and his friends had teased him by saying he was so anxious to break something that he had managed to invent a bone that did not even exist. He had never been one to make a fuss about pain, Nicola Bastíu. Giannina would have been much happier if he had, because seeing him silent and hostile in bed with his stump sewn up

94

and covered by a sheet, burned inside her like a ball of hot fat that refused to dissolve, and rolled up and down while she remade his bed, brought him something to eat or simply looked in to see if there was anything he wanted. They had moved the television into his room to distract him when there was no-one to keep him company, but Nicola hardly ever turned it on and preferred to look out of the window, inhabiting a world of silent rage in which he was the only citizen with an official right of residence. This was how the priest found him when Giannina, overcoming her reluctance, plucked up the courage to follow Bonaria's advice and asked him to come and pay her son a visit.

Vicar of Soreni for the last twenty-one years, Don Frantziscu Pisu had a round belly over which the buttons of his cassock strained mightily every time he took a deep breath. This embarrassing embonpoint contrasted strongly with the rest of his physique which was dry and almost spindly, so that in profile he looked like a lizard that had swallowed an egg, entirely spoiling the austere elegance of his well-worn cassock. At Soreni, everyone smiled at his nervous tic of constantly passing his hands over his belly to smooth down his cassock in an attempt to minimize what he considered his only visible reason for shame.

Even the most good-natured people had taken to mangling his name to *Pisittu* or Pussycat, perhaps because this obsessive action reminded them of the patient licking of a cat smoothing its fur. But some, less charitably inclined, called him *Tzicu*, which was not only a diminutive form of his name but also meant 'little drop', hinting at alcoholic origins for his swollen stomach. He was familiar with both nicknames, but with the patient superiority of one who for more than twenty years had conducted every funeral, even of the disrespectful, he had never taken too much notice. Probably such thoughts were not a million miles from his mind when he knocked on the front door of the Bastíus, a family of men who had most certainly never risked breaking a bone by stumbling up the steps into the church. Even so, he was not entirely amazed when Giannina Bastíu asked him to call on her eldest son, because it would not have been the first time that some self-styled priest-eater had been exposed as God-fearing *in extremis*. When they face crucifixion, all thieves become good men.

'How are you, Nicola?' Don Frantziscu said, entering the bedroom with the furtive encouragement of Giannina, who was careful to keep out of range of any predictable darts from her son.

Nicola moved his eyes from the window and fixed them on the door with the instinctive gesture of a hunter. It took him an instant to focus on the identity of his visitor, but he was not put out.

'Well, well, so they've sent in the priest. Then I must be dying, though I already thought I was crippled for life because I've never learnt to read or write.'

'The fact is, you're not dying, and the doctors will certainly have made that clear to you. I've only come to say hello.'

The young man did not invite the priest to sit down, nor did the older exploit his seniority by sitting down uninvited. Perhaps it was not even the right sort of interview for sitting down, after all.

'What a surprise. I don't think you've ever come to see me before?'

Don Frantziscu showed no embarrassment at the question. With a slow gesture he removed his blue woollen skullcap from his white hair, ignoring Nicola's grimace of annoyance.

'You've never needed me to.'

'What makes you think I need you now? If it was my mother who said so, she was wasting your time.'

'I don't need anyone to tell me; priests do these things on their own initiative, it's their duty.'

'Yes of course, meddling in other people's troubles. A fine duty, which will certainly ensure you a place in paradise. But don't hope, Don Frantzí, that just because I've lost a leg I must need a crutch.'

The old priest well remembered that impudence, that restless intelligence. He searched the eyes of the young man before him, pushing aside his vivid memory of a different Nicola Bastíu, a hostile little boy in short trousers who once grazed his knees on the concrete behind the church. It was easy to recognize the root, seeing the fruit that had grown from it. He sighed quietly.

'I only came to have a word with you, Nicola.'

'To have a word with me? About what, the sex of the angels? Or how to organize the festival of the Maddalena? There's nothing we can't talk about, is there? After all, I've got all the time in the world now.'

'I've come to talk about what happened to you.'

Nicola's response was as scornful as a whiplash:

'You know nothing about what happened to me.'

'You're wrong, at Soreni even the dogs know, just as they know that recklessness cost you your leg.'

98

'Good, then they have something new to discuss in the bar, not just who their wives might be sleeping with. As for you, if you must bless me, get on with it, then go away. Having time to waste doesn't mean I want to waste it with you.'

The priest did not move, standing still beside the door, cap in hand like a beggar. Nicola stared at him, waiting.

'I haven't come to bless you. Blessings are never forced on anyone.'

'Then what? No need to curse me either, as you can see for yourself.'

'Don't blaspheme, your life isn't a curse, even if you have lost a leg. That's what I want to talk to you about.'

Nicola's eyes were like fire and his face was paler and even angrier than his mother had ever seen it in recent days.

'You want to talk to me about my life? Well, priest, and what can you know about that? Are you by any chance living without a limb?' He smiled scornfully, lowering his gaze to Don Frantziscu's level. 'Of course, I know you're short of a limb in one sense, or at least you took a vow to make do without it. It's easy to say 'I'm a cripple by vocation', when what's not being used is still there in case you change your mind.' Nicola stretched forward a little from his pillows, and for a moment the old priest was relieved that he could not get out of bed. 'But I'm in no position to change my mind. And I assure you, you haven't the least idea what I'm talking about.'

Don Frantziscu did not interrupt and gave no sign of wanting to. He had learned long ago that even the least appeal may bring success to a petitioner who expects nothing, and in any case Nicola did not seem to expect any reaction to what had been a clear invitation to end the interview. So he was astonished when the old man, so far from leaving, spoke again:

'Well then, if I've got it right, you've decided to blame everyone who still has two legs, quite apart from demanding sympathy so long as the Lord allows you the breath to feel sorry for yourself.' He scratched his head with a distracted air as if reflecting. 'It's quite normal, Nicola. Many react like this, and they are usually people who lack the comfort of faith, or reject it.'

'Don Frantziscu, say no more,' Nicola's voice was calm now, submissive. 'Don't take advantage of the fact that you're a guest in my father's house.'

The priest was unruffled by this scarcely veiled threat, his eyes fixed on the young man in the middle of the bed. He went on talking in a patient tone, articulating his words as clearly as if talking to a child.

'It is written that one should speak at convenient moments but also when it is not convenient, so I shall speak; and after I've gone you will have plenty of time to reflect on your suffering and what it means. A suffering that to some extent, and don't forget this, you have after all brought on yourself by causing distress to others, but which nevertheless it has not been granted to you to change, except by accepting suffering like Christ our Saviour himself, who suffered unjustly on the cross . . . '

'Get out!'

An angry shout, instantly backed up by a pillow not aimed straight enough to find its mark. Nicola Bastíu was beside himself with fury.

'Calm down, my son . . . '

'I'm not your son, at least I hope not, you swollen cassock! I don't need to listen to your mockery. Just go away! Get out!'

A moment later Giannina Bastíu arrived in response to the cries of her son, just in time to see the priest calmly replacing his skullcap on his head.

'Take Don Tzicu to the door, Mamma. He's in a hurry and has to get away.'

Pretending not to have come specially in response to the disturbance, the mother made a point of showing embarrassed good manners.

'Don Frantziscu, must you go so soon? I haven't even offered you anything.'

'Don't worry, Giannina, in any case it's nearly time for me to say Mass.'

Nicola kept silent while his mother and the old priest left the room. He made no effort to hear whatever they may have said to one another in the corridor, closing his eyes as he searched for some simulacrum of sleep to dampen his rage even if only for an hour.

10

Working together, Giannina Bastíu's hands ran over the limp skin of Nicola's right thigh with hypnotic regularity. In the courtyard behind the house, the weak October sun drew attention to the final flowering of the hydrangeas, while the chrysanthemums budding along the wall stood erect like promises still to come true.

Having just eaten, in the warmest hour of the day, an indifferent Nicola allowed his mother to apply the medicinal massage necessary to keep him free of sores and help his healing. The months of convalescence had gone better than could have been expected, and the suture on his amputated stump had healed without complications. Like a change of seasons, Nicola's attitude seemed to have changed too after the first weeks of blind rage. He no longer cursed and had stopped insulting everyone who came to see him, and there were fewer and fewer moments of fury when he threw objects at random. But he did not speak. He had not grown dumb; it was just that he no longer said anything that was not strictly necessary, and had suddenly stopped reacting to the circumstances round him. Every day his father and brother lifted him out of bed, sat him in a chair and carried him out to the courtyard, without his even having to try to support himself on his good leg. It was only when Bonaria Urrai came to see him that he seemed to shake himself out of his unhealthy torpor, fixing the elderly seamstress with two black eyes like extinguished stars. During these visits he seemed less unreachable, but still had little to say. Bonaria came every day, but she never tried to draw him into any conversation, restricting herself to exchanging a little chatter with Giannina, and looking now and then at Nicola. If she was sure she would find Andría at home, Maria would sometimes go with Bonaria on these visits, but would avoid being left with Nicola, overcome by an unconquerable distaste for that suffering that was no longer even pain. She had sometimes argued with the old woman not to have to go there, because she could see no sense in these forced visits; on the one hand Nicola never gave her any reason to think they were welcome, and on the other Maria preferred spending her afternoons at home, sewing clothes from the paper patterns that arrived by way of business each month, or going to Maestra Luciana's house to ask if she could

104

borrow a book to read in the evening. On this particular afternoon she had clearly not had the best of it: in fact she was sitting beside Bonaria with badly hidden impatience, firmly determined not to let her eyes rest on Giannina's delicate work on Nicola.

'Look what lovely weather, son . . . soon it'll be a little cooler, and we'll go and harvest the grapes and you'll be able to taste the new wine.'

Giannina Bastíu seemed inexplicably to have been born again since the operation on her son. Overcoming her initial shame, she had adjusted the rhythms of the household around the new demands made by having an invalid to attend to, and had set herself regular tasks for each hour, regardless of the absence of any signs of gratitude from the patient. That afternoon too, Nicola did not react at all at the mention of the vintage. Bonaria on the other hand smiled, encouraging the conversation with obvious interest, while Giannina dried her hands on a rag and carefully replaced the covers over Nicola's leg.

'Have you taken Chicchinu to sniff the air in the vineyard yet, or are you going to wait till the birds start eating the grapes this year too?'

'They've taken him there once already, but

it seems we need at least another two weeks. We have to hope the weather will hold. Maria, will you come and help us again this year?'

Forced to distract herself from her constant search for distraction, Maria remained vague, because the idea of finding herself once more working beside her sisters did not particularly appeal to her.

'I don't know, Tzia Giannina, there's so much to do, orders for Christmas clothes have already started coming in. I'm afraid even if I work every day it may be too much for me, just imagine if I fail!' She stood up and turned to Nicola. 'In fact, I ought to get back to work now. A pleasure to see you, Nicola.'

Nothing changed in Nicola's expression, as if he had not even heard her taking her leave. His mother tried to compensate for this lack of manners with an embarrassed smile.

'Oh, I'm sure it's been a great pleasure for him too! But he's tired . . . Sometimes having nothing to do can be more tiring than working all day in the fields, or that's what they say. I'll come with you to the door; anyway, I must go and make the coffee. But do have another cake before you go. Did you know they're called *gueffus*, after some knights in the Middle Ages? Your mother told me that, apparently she read it somewhere, I can't remember where.'

Bonaria was not even ten minutes alone with Nicola, but he made full use of the time. As soon as he heard the door close, he seemed to wake so suddenly from his spell of impenetrability that it was as if he had been waiting for that very moment.

'What have you decided?' he whispered anxiously, grabbing her arm like a drowning man.

She firmly shook off his grasp, but spoke calmly.

'There's nothing to decide. What you're asking for can't be done.'

'I can't go on any longer like this. Have you no pity for my condition?' Nicola's voice trembled with desperation, but Bonaria was unmoved.

'We've already discussed it, Nicola. I won't do it.'

Nicola had prepared himself for her resistance with the same determination he would once have applied to setting traps for hares or erecting supports for rows of vines. When you have enough time you can control even your anger. So Bonaria was certain that this time there would be no scenes.

'But you do it when others ask for it. Am I worth less than they are?'

'You've never understood your own life,

Nicola, and you're certainly not in any position to understand mine. Just get it into your head that I can't help you.'

Nicola sighed as if resigned, then changed his tone.

'What would you say if I wanted to marry Maria?' he asked bluntly, leaving her for a moment dumbfounded.

'That would be for Maria to answer. How on earth could I ever decide such a thing?'

Nicola deliberately made the cover slip from his lap to the floor. Supporting himself on the arms of the chair with his hands, he forced himself as far upright as he could. With this parody of standing to attention he seemed to be challenging Bonaria to look at his exposed stump, still red from the amputation.

'Look at me, Tzia, look at my leg: why play games with reality? Maria would never marry me, nor would anyone else, because I'm a cripple. I'll never be able to work or support a family, or do any of the things a woman needs from a man.' His voice, calm to begin with, gradually grew more tense. 'It's like I was already dead.'

In recent months his body had lost weight and tone, but he was otherwise healthy and his will seemed as strong as ever. Perhaps that was the real problem. If his spirit had been broken, perhaps he could have resigned himself to his condition. Instead there was something obsessive about his determination; in every way he was the same as he had always been. Whether she liked it or not, Nicola Bastíu was one of the most vigorously alive creatures Bonaria had ever seen, though she did not admit this when she turned back to him.

'You're alive to your mother, and she wants the benefits of life for you.'

'My mother's only happy when she has someone to look after. She wants to see me as a child again, but that's no reason for me to stay in this world.'

'It would kill her, and your father too.'

'They'll die anyway, and who'll care about me after that? Will my brother's wife wipe my arse for me? And what woman will marry him when she realizes she'll be inheriting the care of a cripple as well?'

Bonaria closed her eyes. If Giannina Bastíu had come in at that moment she would have assumed the old woman had dozed off in the sun, bored with Nicola's lack of conversation. But she shook her head and opened her eyes again, ever vigilant.

'Even if I wanted to do what you're asking me, I could never do it without the consent of your family.'

Nicola's face lit up; it was as if he had

sensed the vague shadow of a possibility. He relaxed from his tiring upright position and settled back comfortably again in his chair, leaving the cover on the ground. The indecent display of his stump, so inconsistent with his previous rejection of his mutilation, contained the calculated use of a psychological weapon. He could have been a marvellous soldier, Nicola, or a criminal of the highest class.

'I'd never even ask for their consent, but if you were agreeable, there would be a way of avoiding having to ask them.'

'There is no such way, and even if there were I'd have nothing to do with it.' Bonaria's words were final, but her eyes seemed to be asking a question, and Nicola sensed encouragement.

'The night of All Saints. When the door's left open for the dinner for the dead souls, you'd be able to go in and out without anyone suspecting anything! In the morning they'll find me dead in bed and think I've had an accident.'

Bonaria got up quickly and bent down to pick up the coverlet and rearrange it over his legs. This almost intimate position enabled Nicola to grasp her wrist again, this time with insinuating gentleness. He did not speak, and Bonaria responded to his silence with a murmur:

'You're asking me to compromise myself before God and man. You must be out of your mind, Nicola.'

'I've never been more sane than I am today. You may be able to accept the idea of seeing me live the rest of my life as a worm, but it would be three times harder for me. If you help me, my death will pass for natural causes. If not, I'll find a way of my own.'

Whatever Nicola may have hoped, Bonaria Urrai had never for an instant considered the idea of agreeing to what he wanted until that moment. But now she wavered for the first time, because she had heard such words once before, long ago, when behind the hill known as Mont'e Mari there had still been a wood and a time of youth and promise.

★   ★   ★

The war that would later be known as the Great War had already earned its name, summoning from Soreni no less than three levies of men to the trenches of the Piave, and even so many had not been enough. Those discharged seriously wounded from the front brought back news of the heroism of the Sassari Brigade and, at the age of twenty, Bonaria had already seen enough of the world to know that the word 'hero' was the masculine singular of the word 'widow'. Even so, she liked to imagine herself a bride as she lay on the grass beneath the pines, breathing deeply the resinous perfume of the soil and pressing the curly head of Raffaele Zincu to her breast.

Raffaele was not strictly speaking handsome, though every woman of marriageable age in Soreni had dreamed of him as her husband. If the truth be told, some women who already had husbands dreamed of him too because, although there were richer or taller men, no-one at twenty had eyes of that sharp, mocking green that could pierce the eyes of others as if regardless of any price that might have to be paid later. Raffaele's lower lip was as soft as a woman's, and his wayward and sensual character could make girls blush even to speak to him. It meant nothing to Bonaria that the arrogant line of his jaw contained a warning that his passing fancies might not always have entirely innocent consequences. Ever since childhood he had worked together with dozens of others on Taniei Urrai's land, harvesting melons in summer and olives in winter with an energy that had earned him the respect of his employer and his companions. Whoever knocked down the olives with Raffaele would finish the day first and best, and old Urrai often boasted of the results at supper, insisting that Raffaele was a superman in hand and word; Bonaria, who also knew of other superior qualities in Raffaele, would agree with carefully calculated stinginess. Where her father counted vines she counted pines, and if he dreamed of seas of golden ears of corn she was able to run her hand through a field of dark curls on certain Saturday afternoons when her father was not there, and no war would ever be able to extinguish Raffaele's fire in her blood. They did talk, sometimes for hours, about the possibility he might be called up to the front, but Raffaele always assumed he would come home again.

'Will you still want me if I come back like Vincenzo Bellu?'

'With only one arm? Of course, because they'll give you the Order of Vittorio Veneto and I'll be your lady!' Bonaria had laughed softly and lightly touched his ears.

'I'm not joking. Would you still want me if I was a cripple? Deafened by a grenade or with no legs like Luigi Barranca?'

'I'd want you back in any condition, as long as you were still alive.'

Bonaria's unconditional reply had not reassured him. At such times his voice had been darker than usual.

'Maybe you can imagine having me back as

a worm, but I'd rather die full of life ten times over than have to live ten years like a dead man. If that happens to me I shall do what Barranca did and shoot myself.'

'Never let me hear you say that, Arrafiei.'

Bonaria had not even dared to look up at the sky as she put her hand over his mouth to stop his words, and pulled his head on to her lap. As she gazed at him in that peaceful shade, he seemed more perfect than ever, so vibrant with vitality that even his healthy body, intact in every part, could not contain it.

'They'll never call you up, just wait and see,' she had said as if pronouncing an exorcism.

'Who knows, but if I do go, you must pray for me to come back. Then when I get home, I'll see to everything else myself.'

But they did call him up, and Bonaria had had to spend thirty-five years praying for him, because no-one ever did come back to Soreni to report that the son of Lizio Zincu had been a hero in the trenches.

★   ★   ★

When Giannina Bastíu returned with a tray of steaming coffee, she found Nicola alone in the sun with three empty chairs and a strange smile on his face.

114

11

The souls know us, they are our own relatives so they will not hurt us, and we have even prepared a feast for them. This was what Andría Bastíu was thinking while he was getting ready in his room for the night of the first of November. He took off his outdoor shoes but did not undress since he had no intention of going to sleep. The previous year his mother had deliberately made him spend all day lifting potatoes to tire him out, so that in the evening he had fallen asleep despite himself, betrayed by his body. But this time they had not tricked him; he was awake and would be able to watch the spirits eating and taking the tobacco cut up for them from the table, where in the morning fingermarks would be found. So he would know what to say to Maria when she claimed the souls never go around tormenting people, because the mercy of Our Lord Jesus Christ did not allow it. If Our Lord Jesus Christ had allowed his brother to lose a leg, surely he would not prevent the dead eating a couple of *culurgiones*.

So he had sat down in silence on a little

bench made of rods he had used as a child, with nails which dug into his bottom, keeping an eye on the crack in his door with the determination of a frontier guard. After twenty minutes he was ready to doze off, but he went on crouching behind the half-closed door, his eye firmly on the line of the corridor leading from the front door to the table laid ready with the feast for the dead souls. There were always many souls abroad that night, Nicola had told him, having the previous year even seen the soul of Antoni Juliu, his mother's older brother, walking down the road towards their house. Antoni Juliu had gone as an emigrant to the mines in Belgium, but when he returned he no longer seemed to feel at home: he would look about like someone afraid of his creditors, and never got rid of the black coal dust under his nails. He had been unhappy to go away, and was even less happy to be back. The third summer he had hanged himself on the Gongius' family farm, shocking the sharecroppers who found him hanging from a branch like a rotten pear with his tongue sticking out, having emigrated from himself to heaven knew where.

Maybe Antoni Juliu really would come that night. A dish had been prepared for him with a small glass of *abbardente* beside it, because he had been fond of *eau de vie*, rather too

116

fond in fact. If he did not come and drink it, Andría's father would drink it before dinner, or Nicola who, God knows, had need of it. But that black figure heading down the corridor like a curse could not be the soul of Antoni Juliu, passing Andría's door with a swish of skirts. That head in its black scarf could not possibly be that of his uncle, that firm step was of someone who had never been forced to leave this earth.

When Andría saw the mysterious figure come into the house he closed his eyes in disbelief, tormented by the discrepancy between faith and fact. Were there dead females in the family? He wanted to close his door at once, slamming it hard and beating against it with his fear, but the soul would have been too close not to notice. But luckily the figure stopped just after his room, in front of Nicola's door. Andría saw it enter, then took a short breath, and in what he hoped was perfect silence performed the first reckless act of his life, and left his room to go into the corridor.

★ ★ ★

On a night like this night of souls, the church bell did not toll. It could have been any hour, but nothing would have been any different.

All along the streets the house doors were open in spite of the cold, as if every family in Soreni had run away so quickly that they had forgotten to close their front door. More in her element on this night than any other in the year, the tall woman close to the wall walked down the street with the step of one who knew exactly where she was going. She moved quickly, wrapped in a dark shawl, until her skirts touched the threshold of the Bastíu house. Then she slipped soundlessly down the corridor leaving no memory of herself in the street. In that house she moved even at night with the confident step of a member of the family, passing the rooms to reach the only door she knew would not be shut, the one behind which Nicola Bastíu, stupefied by pain and expectation, was stealing a moment of sleep.

Nicola was dreaming of the sea, the sea he had known for twenty years, the only sea he had ever seen. Eight years earlier he had rolled up his trousers and immersed himself in it up to his chest, letting the hard salt water strike him. His cousins were surfing the waves and hurling the water-melon as if they were back home in the hay. But Nicola had stared wide-eyed at the horizon where the sea ended, and the more he gazed at it, the more he wanted to retreat slowly backwards to the

118

shore, without running or turning round, as one does when faced with certain snakes. Now in his dream it was as if he were back on that Easter Monday, but the sand on the sea bottom was much stickier, a boneless monster that would not let him walk. If only he could have died like this, drowning in the water of his dreams, it would have been better for everyone. But he suddenly opened his eyes, groping in his crippled state among the sheets. It took him a few moments to remember who he was and what was happening, since the more deeply you sleep the more difficult it is to wake. It was some time before he became aware of the thin figure impinging on the air of the room, motionless by the wall at the foot of his bed. Nicola had never been a man of many words, but in that moment not even silence seemed appropriate.

'You've come . . . ' he whispered, hoarse and pale.

The woman approached the bed, but it was only when she came close that Nicola was reminded that she seemed to bring with her the bitter smell of the old. When she spoke, he knew he was fully awake.

'I've come, but I can also go away again. Tell me you've changed your mind and I'll go and not look back. I swear we'll never speak of it again, as if nothing had ever happened.'

Nicola answered rather too quickly, as if afraid to allow time for doubts.

'I haven't changed my mind. I'm already dead, and you know it.'

She looked straight into his eyes, moving her head to force him to hold her gaze. She found what she did not want to find and said in a tired voice:

'No, Nicola, I don't know it. Only you can know that. I've come as I promised, but pray to the Lord to grant you what you are asking of me, because it is unholy and not even necessary.'

'It is necessary for me,' said Nicola, acknowledging the curse with a slight movement of his head.

The *accabadora* reached out from under her shawl, her hands holding tightly a small earthenware pot with a wide opening. When she lifted its lid a thread of smoke rose from the pot. Nicola became aware of an acrid smell, not that he expected anything different, took a deep breath and murmured words the old woman showed no sign of having heard. He held the poisonous fumes in his lungs and closed his eyes, anaesthetized for the last time. He may have already been asleep when the pillow was pressed down on his face, because he did not move or struggle. Perhaps he would not have fought back in any case, since for him it would have only made sense to die in the same way as he had lived: breathlessly.

★ ★ ★

Andría Bastíu, cold with terror and watching through the crack in the door, saw the black female soul talking with his brother, then bending over him with the pillow in her hands. That was not what souls came to do. Or was it? Perhaps that was why his mother had said the door must be closed, and closed firmly, not left ajar because the dead can envy your breath and may suddenly come and steal it away in a pillow. And the dinner is set out to distract them, not to please them. They eat until dawn; in the darkness in the house they mistake the sauce of the *culurgiones* for blood, and the meat of the sucking-pig for red thighs and cheeks, and they never realize that there are living people behind the other doors, unless someone reminds them. And in that moment Andría knew that, if he survived, he would never touch a *curlugione* in his life again.

When the figure of the female soul near Nicola's bed moved to replace the pillow under his head, Andría retreated blindly into the corridor miming with his lips fragments of the *Pater ave gloria*, which he had never known well. It was only by accident that he managed not to break the silence that had been his protection, managing to separate himself from the apparition with the insubstantial thickness of the door of his room. As he was carefully closing it, he caught sight of the figure walking quickly towards the way out. An aunt, a grandmother, the drowned sister of his mother, he no longer wanted to know who it was, but he was not quick enough to escape finding out: a ray of moonlight from the open front door was all it needed for Andría Bastíu to recognize in the tear-streaked face of the woman hurrying down the corridor the unmistakable features of Bonaria Urrai. Then night returned, for real.

12

Like owls' eyes, some thoughts cannot tolerate the full light of day. Such thoughts can only be born at night, when they work like the moon, moving tides of feeling to some invisible distant part of the soul. Bonaria Urrai had many thoughts of this kind, and over the years had learnt how to control them, patiently choosing on which nights to let them surface. The *accabadora* shed only a few tears as she left the Bastíu house, burdened though she was by Nicola's breathing, but each tear cut a new furrow in her already well-lined face. Had the sun risen at that moment, Bonaria Urrai would have appeared many years older than she actually was, and she was certainly feeling the weight of every one of those extra years. Decades had passed since she had first responded to a deathbed plea for peace, but she could confidently claim that neither then nor later had she ever felt anything to equal the weight now hanging from her like a wet cloak.

She had a clear memory of that first time, when she was not yet fifteen. With the other women of the family she had been present at the home confinement of a cousin of her father, thirteen hours of labour which cost the mother more than her baby, who was born alive. Neither chicken broth nor prayers had been able to stop the woman's bleeding, which was followed by days of such suffering as to extinguish any hope of recovery. This being the case, the room was emptied of every holy object, every well-wisher's present and every religious picture, so that the things which had been intended so far to protect the woman during childbirth did not now lock her into a state of eternal suffering. When she begged for mercy the others had reacted in an atmosphere of shared naturalness, when doing nothing would have seemed more like doing wrong. No-one ever explained this to Bonaria, but it had been obvious to her that the women had ended the mother's suffering with the same logic as they had used when they cut the child's umbilical cord.

That first bitter practical lesson taught the daughter of Taniei Urrai the unwritten law that the only accursed state was dying or being born alone, and that her own perfectly acceptable function had been just to stand by and watch. At fifteen years of age Bonaria had already been able to understand that with some things, doing them yourself or watching others do them involves the same degree of guilt, and from then on she had never had any problem distinguishing between compassion and crime. At least, not until that evening, when what she read in the eyes of Nicola Bastíu was not determination to find peace, but determination to find an accomplice.

No souls visited the house of Bonaria Urrai that night, but her door stayed open till morning, when the tolling of the death bells woke Soreni from the torpor of sleep. Maria found the old woman sitting with her eyes fixed on the spent hearth, bound up in her black shawl like a spider trapped in her own web.

★ ★ ★

When they came to tell Frantziscu Pisu that there had been a death in the Bastíu home, his first thought was that the head of the family must have had a stroke. The whole village had been saying that old Salvatore had been in a decline for months since the accident to his eldest son and, though he pretended to Nicola that everything could be fixed, when he was out drinking with his friends he bitterly mourned the loss of his son, now dead in every respect that made a man's life worthwhile. For weeks this had been the only subject of discussion in the bars, and on the doorsteps at sunset. Nothing had helped Salvatore imagine any acceptable future for his son because, just as iron cannot be made from wood, the worst curse old Bastíu could imagine was being still alive with people referring to one in the past tense.

Knowing that this was the way things stood, when Don Tzicu learnt that the dead man was Nicola, he made a gesture halfway between the sign of the cross and an exorcism and, heading for the house, felt too late a guilty conscience for not having more effectively persuaded young Bastíu to accept his condition as a mystery of the divine will. In fact, though he was convinced that half the things in life were mysteries of the divine will, Frantziscu Pisu knew very well that the other half were clearly the fruit of human stupidity; and what had happened to Nicola Bastíu was surely best explained by the second hypothesis. An inability to lie was the most obvious of Frantziscu Pisu's failings, and for a priest this was not a negligible defect. Certainly, if he had known that Nicola would die like this, he would probably have put a little more effort into his lying, but who could imagine the poor man had so displeased heaven as to suffer the misfortune of dying in his sleep? Even among those with such short memories as to believe their consciences were in good shape, there was no-one who did not hope for the last-minute redemption of the thief on the cross, and the elderly priest who, to be fair to him, did have quite a good memory, recited a *Pater noster* with the heartfelt fervour of an exorcism.

Only the closest members of the family were there in the corridor, and the body had not yet been prepared for the procession of mourners that would fill the house with cries and weeping during the next few hours; there was an atmosphere of shock and incompleteness, emphasized by the table still laid for the dead and easily visible from the corridor, which made it clear to everyone that death had taken the family by surprise. Giannina, paralysed by grief, was in Nicola's open room and was not even wearing black; when she saw the priest come in she showed no trace of her customary politeness, and went on sitting in silence by the bed, her hand in the dead hand of her son, which was cold but still soft. It was Salvatore Bastíu who received the priest; Don Frantziscu saw him come forward, pale and awkward, with no trace of his usual arrogance, like an innocent man just handed a severe sentence.

'Thank you for coming, Don Frantziscu. I'm sure a good word will be a great help to

Giannina in this misfortune . . . '

The priest nodded, took off his skullcap and began to move tactfully towards the woman beside the bed. It was only then that he noticed someone else in the room. Andría Bastíu was standing back to the wall in the corner behind the door, with his hands behind his back and his gaze fixed on the bed where the motionless body of his brother was lying. The boy nodded stiffly to the priest, fixing him with feverish sleepless eyes.

'Giannina . . . ' Don Frantziscu turned gently to the woman, who spoke as if answering a question.

'He wasn't a bad boy, Nicola, he was a good son.'

'I know, Giannina, I know.'

'Then bless him for me . . . so the Lord can accept him as he is, because he wasn't a bad boy, my son . . . '

As she spoke, Giannina Bastíu lost something of the calm she had preserved until that moment, letting silent tears fall from her eyes. Don Frantziscu draped a purple stole round his neck and began to pray as a respectful form of distraction. While the priest was inflicting on the defenceless corpse what Nicola would never have accepted alive, Andría abruptly went out of the room, leaving his mother to console herself with the rhythmical Latin of the prayers. He waited outside with his father until the priest came out, listening in silence to their conversation.

'Is it known what happened?' Don Frantziscu said.

Old Bastíu shook his head in bewilderment. 'Dr Mastinu has spoken of a heart attack. To me that doesn't seem possible. If any part of my son was still in good shape, it was his heart.'

'The Lord never gathers unripe fruit, Salvatore. We all leave when the time is ripe for us to depart. Be strong.'

'I'm not short of strength, Don Frantziscu. It's just that pain's an ugly thing, and you can't know that until you feel it.'

'Be comforted in the knowledge that he is better off where he is now.'

To crown this series of trite remarks, the priest turned to Andría, who had not responded positively to any of his invitations to resign himself. Like a shadow at Salvatore's shoulder, the lad seemed to be waiting for something.

'Now that you are the only one left, you must be a comfort to your mother and father.'

'Maybe when I've managed to comfort myself,' Andría said drily.

His father stared at him, surprised by his tone, but the look he got back discouraged him from venturing reproach on a day when uncontrolled speech could find easy justification. The priest tried to insist, but Andría's attention had already been drawn over his shoulder as he caught sight of someone crossing the threshold at that moment. Turning to see what he was looking at, Don Frantziscu Pisu recognized among the new arrivals the tall gaunt figure of Bonaria Urrai and the slender one of Maria Listru, and it suddenly occurred to him that this presented him with an ideal opportunity to escape. Maria greeted him warmly as he left, but Bonaria Urrai barely deigned to glance at him as she headed for the dead man and his mother to do what she had come to do.

Two hours later, when the procession of formal visits began, Nicola was ready to receive them, carefully laid out on the bed in the best suit that Bonaria Urrai herself had made him two years earlier for the feast of San Giacomo. It was impossible to tell the amputated leg in its carefully stuffed trouser from the other, and Nicola's well-shaved face had such a serene and relaxed expression as to give Maria the impression that at long last he was welcoming visitors. No professional *attittadora* had been engaged for this vigil, but all the same many of the women who arrived dressed in black wept with loud cries, while the men waited outside for the end of this formal display of grief, before coming in to offer the family their more restrained expressions of sympathy.

At Luvè and Illamari, which both aspired to the status of towns, it had become increasingly common not to wear black for a death, and it had been noticed ever more frequently that the more well-to-do and cultured families were dispensing with visits from mourners, but at Soreni no-one considered themselves to have yet reached such a peak of civilization as to be able to dispense with the solidarity of their fellows when a member of the family died, or not to wear black in their honour. For Maria, born to a father already dead, black was her natural everyday colour. Those who are born orphans learn from birth to live with absence, and Maria had got the idea that mourning, like such absences, should last for ever. It was only as she got older that she began to notice the wives and daughters of some people who had died changing their clothes with the changing seasons.

Years earlier, one sunny afternoon much like the present one, when Tzia Bonaria was beginning to teach her to sew things suitable for a child, Maria had asked her to explain these wardrobe earthquakes.

'When does mourning end, Tzia?'

The old woman never even raised her head from the pinafore she was putting the finishing touches to.

'What questions you ask! When grief is past, mourning is over.'

'So mourning helps to show that there is grief,' Maria had said, trying to understand, as the conversation faded away in the slow silence of needle and thread.

'No, Maria, that's not the reason for mourning. Grief is naked, and black serves to cover it, to hide it.' She had watched the child for a moment, then smiled at her. 'The flower you've sewn is crooked, let me have a look . . . '

Maria had heard these words as an incomprehensible warning, but she often remembered them in the years that followed, as she noticed some people change the expression in their eyes more quickly than their clothes, while the rapid steps of false shame could turn to dancing with the dead person still warm in the house. On the other hand, when she saw Giannina Bastíu crouched beside her son in a gaudy flowered dress without a sign of black on it, Maria understood clearly that this was a woman in deeper mourning than anyone else who had lamented a death at Soreni, and she finally understood what Bonaria had been trying to explain. Needing fresh air, she made a sign to Tzia and went out, turning her back on the women whimpering through the rosary for the dead like a lullaby.

Andría was outside with the men. When he saw her he broke away and came to meet her.

'Andrí, how terrible, I don't know what to say.'

'Then at least you can say nothing, because I've heard enough rubbish for one day.'

Maria looked at her friend, astonished at his angry language, but she did not dare to make any comment. She would have preferred to change the subject, but finding nothing more suitable than silence, kept quiet. It was he who counter-attacked.

'Are you coming with us to the vineyard to harvest the grapes next week?'

'Don't talk nonsense, Andría. Your brother's dead, and unless his friends harvest them for him, your father will leave the bunches to rot on the vines.' Maria was too disconcerted to be tactful.

'That's the last thing Nicola would have wanted.' As he spoke Andría gave a light kick to a stone, sending it to knock as if tired against the opposite wall.

'There are some things Nicola would have wanted . . . but the grape-harvest's a festival, and since when do we celebrate festivals when someone has just died?' Maria tried to temper her refusal: 'I'll help you all next year.'

'Next year . . . ' murmured Andría almost inaudibly, staring fixedly at his foot.

Maria waited impatiently for him to raise his eyes, but he did not do so. He stood motionless to one side of the housefront, staring at the ground as if he had lost something, trembling slightly. Maria knew what was about to happen, because she and Andría had grown up together, and while it had been a considerable problem between them, it was useful sometimes to be the first to detect even such subtle signs as this.

'Let's get away from here, let's go to the yard, come on . . . '

Maria put her arm through his and led him quickly through the house, carefully avoiding the place where the formal lamentation for Nicola was going on. They only just reached the courtyard in time. Andría placed one hand on the wall, bent over and vomited, not even bothering to move his legs apart so as not to soil his shoes. He was shaken by what seemed to Maria an endless succession of spasms, and did not raise his head till there was no bile left in him, closing his eyes and flushed with effort. They had been unobserved.

'Feeling better? Wash your face in the basin, come on . . . '

Andría did not bother to pretend that he felt better, but he went to the concrete bath for washing clothes without arguing, and turned on the tap to do as he was told. As he washed his face in the icy water lucidity returned to him. Deep down, in all those years, that was all he had done: he had obeyed Maria, listened to Maria, and paid attention to Maria. He had been happy to do so, because Maria was intelligent and decent; and had only ever asked him to do things that made sense for him. If Nicola had had a woman like Maria at his side, he would never have set fire to Manuele Porresu's farm, and would not now have been lying at home on his back as cold as a frog, with twenty old women in black singing over him. As the water dripped from his face, Andría lifted his eyes and looked at Maria, she too dressed in black for the occasion, but as beautiful as if her clothes had been the colour of geraniums, or white like a bride's. In Andría's eyes, in all Soreni no other girl could even come near Maria for beauty, and his brother had always known that without any need for Andría to confide in him. 'Have you told Maria Urrai that you've fallen in love with her, or shall I have to go and write it on the wall of her house?' Even with two litres of *eau de vie* inside him, Andría would never have had the courage to tell Maria his feelings, and Nicola knew that perfectly well, but had never let on to anyone about it, because he had concerns of his own to think about; first he had to go and set fire to a farm, and then hurry to lose his leg, and then lose his will to live too, and finally lose his breath under a pillow, because fire can cause that and other things as well, it goes on burning after it has gone out, did you not know that, Maria? Have you never seen fire really burning?

'What are you talking about, Andrí?'

He had not even been aware he was speaking aloud, but now that he realized it, he saw no reason not to go on. With a sleepless night behind him, and grief gnawing at his belly, he said:

'Maria, will you be my wife?'

She looked at him as if contemplating some slow-drying laundry, and with a practical gesture handed him a towel.

'If I hadn't just seen the contents of your stomach, I'd swear you were drunk. Dry yourself.'

'I'm not drunk, I've never been more sober than I am now,' he said, grabbing the towel. When his dried face emerged from the towel, he looked at her again and took courage. 'Will you marry me?'

'If you're being serious, the answer is no.

For the same reason that I wouldn't marry my sister Regina.' She was obviously not taking him seriously, and this was also familiar to Andría. Tiresomely familiar.

'You don't believe a word I say. You're treating me like someone incapable of understanding.'

'How do you expect me to treat you, when you ask me to marry you in front of your own vomit and with the dead body of your brother in the house?'

At any other time Andría would have realized that Maria was being perfectly reasonable, but if he had been in a state to follow logic he would have simply kept quiet, and this was not the case.

'And if I ask you again tomorrow with my brother underground, will you answer then or not?'

Maria began to understand that Andría was very far from joking. She turned pale, but played for time.

'I don't think this is a good time to talk about it.'

Andría, who knew her as well as she knew him, recognized her familiar trick of throwing him off the scent and laughed bitterly, because he knew this was a serious answer.

'I've got the point. And I'm a real fool. You really think of me as your sister, you don't even see me as a man.'

'You're just saying one stupid thing after another, Andría, I've never before heard you talk such nonsense.'

'No, I've never understood things more clearly than I do now. It's you who don't understand, and you've never understood my feelings for you.'

Maria was deeply embarrassed. Her friend's suffering was obvious, and she would have done anything else he asked her to help him get over it, even lie. But not on a subject like that.

'When have I ever given you reason to think I was in love with you?'

Andría looked down at his shoes splashed with vomit. 'And why have I never studied? Why did I stop after elementary school?'

'No, what's that got to do with . . . ?'

'But it does matter, as I see it. Maestra Luciana has always told you you're intelligent, that you would do well, that you deserved this or that.'

'Andría, I'm a seamstress. I shall never get engaged to the Prince of Wales. I'm just like you.'

'Then why don't you want me?'

'Because I'm not in love with you. I've always seen myself as your sibling.'

'But I already had a brother!' he said

angrily. Then he added maliciously: 'And now Bonaria Urrai has killed him for me.'

Maria looked at him in astonishment; with his twisted face and reddened eyes Andría seemed to her to have taken leave of his senses. A sense of shame made her look away, almost as if she did not want to risk fixing him in her memory in that state.

'Andrí, you have no idea what you're talking about,' she said, taking back the towel and beginning to fold it.'

'No, I mean it. She killed him.'

There was something in his insistence that worried Maria. She set aside her scruples and again concentrated her eyes on him, also removing the increasing hardness from her voice.

'That's enough. Feeling unwell is no excuse for disrespect.'

She turned her back on him to go back into the house, but he had no intention of letting her have the last word with a triumphant rebuke. He caught up with her with a sudden movement and grabbed her arm.

'Let me go. You stink of vomit.'

'No, not till you listen to me. Ask Tzia Bonaria where she went last night,' he said, glassy-eyed, putting his face close to hers.

'To bed, like everyone else,' Maria said bluntly.

'Oh no, my little beauty. Not everyone. I was awake and I saw her. She came here and killed my brother by pressing a pillow on his face.'

Maria responded with a look colder than Andría had ever seen from her, making him feel less than a worm. He immediately wished he could have run time backwards and eaten every word he had said.

'She came here?' Maria said slowly.

Andría immediately let go of her arm and took one step back, then another.

'No, she never came here . . . Excuse me. I don't know what I'm saying.' He was stammering, avoiding her eyes.

This denial alarmed Maria more than a confirmation would have done. She bridged the distance he was trying to create between them, pressing him.

'Tell me what you saw.'

It was a command, and in that moment Andría knew he had passed the point at which he could have retreated and set things to rights. Crushed by his own superficiality, he let himself slip to the ground and explained in tears everything that had happened the previous night while Maria listened in disbelief, neither of them aware that in that house a funeral lament was in progress for not one but three deaths: the life of Nicola, the innocence of Andría, and Maria Listru's trust in Bonaria Urrai.

Upset by these incomprehensible revelations, Maria left the house without another word. Andría stayed sobbing in the courtyard, his gratified relatives interpreting this as deep grief for the death of his brother.

13

Although immersed in the collective ritual of the mourning, Bonaria Urrai had not failed to notice how precipitately Maria had left the Bastíu house, though she only half understood the reason for this unseemly behaviour. But the old woman could not allow herself the luxury of behaving impulsively on such an occasion, and Nicola Bastíu deserved her respect every inch of the way to his grave. Only now could she honour the secret promises she had made him, while Maria would still be at home when she got back. Thus reasoned the Soreni seamstress as she stayed close to Giannina and Salvatore Bastíu who had always treated her like a member of the family, and she sang the *Requiescat* together with everyone else who happened to be present, as if for her this was a dead person like any other, different only in name.

In fact Nicola's face, relaxed in the artificial serenity of someone who no longer had any questions to ask, seemed finally at peace, but this optical illusion could not arrest the tumult of uncertainty in the soul of Bonaria Urrai. In any case the old woman was so used to never revealing any feelings except those expected of her that she had no difficulty, in the presence of the body, in maintaining her composure just as she had always done over the years, assisting the dead man's parents to concentrate on their many happy memories of him, recreating a healthy, laughing Nicola Bastíu, utterly respectable in body and soul. For several hours the voices of women and men round the corpse alternated in a liturgical sequence of weeping, prayer and memory. None of these sections could be left out of this code essential to the community in repairing the break between presence and absence. By this act of acceptance of individual grief, even the most controversial death could be reconciled with the tragic quality naturally inherent in every life. Thus when the priest left after pontificating on the communion of saints, the people of Soreni came together to celebrate the communion of sinners, absolving the surviving relatives of blame for their unique grief. There would be time later to answer other questions.

★ ★ ★

There are things you should do and things you should not do, and Maria was strongly aware of the difference. It was not a question of being right or wrong, because in her world such categories had no place. At Soreni the word 'justice' was equivalent to the most violent curse, and it was only ever used when someone had to be hunted down at all costs. For the people of Soreni, justice could flay you like a pig or crucify you like a Christ, or fuck you up for fun the way men can when they behave like animals; there was nowhere you could hide from it, and it would never forget your name or the names of any of your children, but all this had nothing to do with the fact that there were some things you should do and some things you should not do.

As she cut the onion into thin slices, Maria mulled obsessively over this difference, arranging the ingredients for supper with the same hypnotic slowness with which she was trying to order her thoughts. Andría's words had been as crazy as the light in his eyes as he was saying them, and they had made no sense to Maria, though when set against certain memories they began to take on some sort of meaning. As she cut the tomato into pieces, the figure of the old seamstress huddled by the fire that very morning came back to trouble her: fully dressed and with her hair done as though she had just returned home, or already knew that she would soon have to go out. Maria had long ago stopped pondering the mysterious nocturnal expeditions of her elderly adoptive mother, but now these suppressed memories came back to hit her as if fired from the elastic of a catapult, prompting the insidious thought that Bonaria Urrai might indeed have something serious to hide. It was the first time such a thought had ever struck Maria, and she did not know how to cope with this suspicion which fitted so badly with the confidence she felt in the woman who had taken her to be her daughter. Bonaria could not possibly have lied to her, because there are things you should do and things you should not do, she reminded herself as she dropped the rest of the finely chopped vegetables into the sizzling oil. The wooden spoon evoked fragrances and memories among the browning onions and, as she slowly stirred them, Maria opened herself to both, and remembered an afternoon from many years before, only a few months after Tzia Bonaria had first taken her as her soul-child.

★   ★   ★

She had not yet got over her bad habit of stealing little things she did not need but wanted to have. The habit had come with her from the home of Anna Teresa Listru, and for a time had continued to keep her company, so that she did not bother to ask permission whenever she could avoid doing so. Sometimes it was a piece of fruit she wanted, or a piece of bread; or it might be a toy, or a scrap of coloured cloth put aside as a trimming. If she thought no-one was looking, Maria would simply take the object and hide it, incapable of separating desire from stealth. Bonaria Urrai very soon became aware of this, partly because these little disappearances happened rather frequently. But this particular afternoon was the last time it happened, and Maria remembered it very clearly.

It had been late October and sweetmeats were being prepared, with the ingredients for the *pabassinos* for the dead left out on the kitchen table, including orange peel, fennel seeds, slices of almond and a jar of *saba* of prickly pear as dark and sticky as caramel with a sweet taste full of flower perfumes, intended to hold the mixture together like an aromatic cement. Each ingredient had its own paper bag, except the raisins which had been put to soften in a bowl of orange-flower water. Bonaria noticed at the last minute that she had run out of bran, absolutely essential to stop the cakes sticking during baking. She had not told Maria not to touch what was on the table before she went out but, perfectly aware she was doing something she should not do, Maria had grabbed two handfuls of almond slices and run into her room to hide them in a drawer. When Bonaria came back with the bran, half the pile of almonds was missing, and Maria was sitting on the floor playing with an expression of serene innocence on her face. Bonaria did not start with an accusation.

'Some almonds are missing.'

Maria had raised her head, looking at Tzia with a questioning expression, which could have been taken as an answer, but Bonaria had no intention of being fobbed off with that.

'Have you touched them?'

'No.'

The slap that caught Maria was violent and accurate, leaving a bloodless imprint on her left cheek. Her eyes wide with disbelief and surprise, the child stared at the old woman with her mouth open, forgetting to cry.

'Get up,' Bonaria said in a serious voice.

Maria got to her feet slowly, her eyes fixed on the floor to hide the deep shame now suffusing her face along with the red mark of the smack. Bonaria grabbed her arm and dragged her unceremoniously to her room. The old woman closed the door on her, and making sure it was properly locked, went back to making the sweets without another word. Maria stayed locked in her room till supper-time, going through a series of activities to distract herself from what she had done: first she cried silently, then tried to play with her toys as if nothing had happened, then finally, frustrated and exhausted, lay down on her bed and even fell asleep. But when the door opened again she was awake, and was sitting on the bed as if waiting for something. Bonaria picked up the chair by the wall and sat down facing Maria directly.

'Do you understand why I hit you?'

Maria had been expecting this question and nodded, once more blushing with humiliation.

'Why?'

'Because I stole the almonds.'

'No.'

Bonaria's categorical denial surprised her, wrecking her personal interpretation of the afternoon's events. She said no more, fastening astonished eyes on the old woman.

'I hit you because you lied to me. I can buy more almonds, but there's no cure for a lie. Every time you open your mouth to speak, remember that it was with words that God created the world.'

At six years of age one's understanding of theology is limited, and Maria could find nothing to say to that statement, which was altogether too vast for her to take in. But what little she did understand of it was more than enough for her to judge herself, and while she tried to nod with her lips pressed together, Bonaria leaned forward and took her loosely in her arms, like a cocoon round a silkworm. After this reconciliation which remained unique in their shared experience, Maria came out of the room hand in hand with the old woman to find the house filled with the intense fragrance of the sweetmeats, by now cooked and spread out to set on the baking tray like little dark bricks. For years she would associate the smell of freshly made *pabassinos* with that memory and, without being aware of the fact, she no longer felt any desire to steal things that were clearly already hers, because once this fact had been established, there was no-one left to lie to.

★ ★ ★

Remembering this, Maria Listru smiled to herself as she added water to the pan where the tomato had by now dissolved into a dense aromatic sauce. Whatever had happened that night, whatever Andría imagined he had seen, by the time the tomato sauce was ready, Maria was convinced that the woman who

149

had taught her to wash her hands before speaking could not have deceived her in any way, least of all in such an important matter. There are things you should do and things you should not do, she told herself; and this is the way you do things you should do, she decided, tasting the sauce to find out whether it needed any salt.

★   ★   ★

Maria was wrong, but she did not know how wrong she was until that evening, when Bonaria came home after one of the most difficult days of her life. Maria had not waited to eat with her, because with births and deaths you know when you go out but you can never be sure when you will be able to come back home, but there was a panful of cold water waiting on the hob and the sauce was still fresh from its first cooking. Maria was reading, as she often did in the evening after supper, and Bonaria was too tired to notice that there was something not quite natural in her manner.

'Why did you go off like that? Have you quarrelled with Andría?'

When she already knew the answer she expected, Bonaria sometimes started with a direct question.

'Yes.'

Maria watched her with an appearance of calm, while measuring with her eyes the exhaustion visible in Bonaria's bowed shoulders, marked face and black skirt disordered after spending so long sitting down. To Maria she looked old in the ordinary sense in which people commonly use the term, near her end like a well-kept promise.

'Did that seem like the right time to go, with his brother dead in the house? You could have comforted him.'

'I did comfort him.'

'It didn't look like that to me. You rushed away.'

If only Bonaria had not been so insistent. If only she had not pressed for an explanation at all costs, perhaps Maria would have gone on thinking this might be a good moment to keep quiet. But the lack of respect in Bonaria's accusations pushed her into answering sharply, moving the conversation into more treacherous waters.

'If I'd stayed it would have been worse. He was saying things I wasn't prepared to listen to.'

'Bereaved people always say the same things. What did he want, did he want to die too? Did he blame himself for Nicola's death?'

Maria closed her book without bothering

to mark her place. When she spoke again, it was with a careful lack of expression.

'No, he didn't blame himself. He blamed you.'

Bonaria kept quite still, and her expression did not change in any way.

'Blamed me? Good heavens! Why?'

'He says he saw you going into Nicola's room last night and suffocating him with a pillow.'

Put like that, if it had not involved Nicola, it might even have sounded funny, and making such an indirect accusation made her aware of the lack of logic in what she was saying. Her reconstruction seemed to make no sense at all. But Bonaria did not laugh.

'He told you that?'

'Yes, exactly that, but then he vomited and said he'd made it up.'

Bonaria Urrai sat down near the fire, carefully adjusting the folds of her skirt round her body, like the petals of a black flower. The conversation was over, but even so Maria felt a need to say something more:

'He was completely beside himself, not making any sense.'

The old woman turned to face the fire, hiding the expression of her eyes in a defensive gesture so unlike her that Maria felt within her a long finger of suspicion without quite knowing what it was she suspected. In a low voice she said,

'Where were you last night?'

Bonaria felt no need to break the silence, letting it be her answer. She kept her eyes fixed on the heavily smoking firewood. But for Maria it was as if Bonaria had replied in a complete sentence. Rising abruptly, she put down her book on the table set for one, going up to the old woman who was again huddled in the position in which she had surprised her that morning.

'You went out, I know you did. Where did you go?'

Bonaria lifted her eyes from the fire, holding Maria's gaze without replying. In her empty eyes Maria saw the shadow of what she did not even know she should fear, and wavered.

'It's not possible.'

'Maria . . . '

'You did do it. You really did go to Nicola last night.' The girl was no longer even asking questions.

'He asked me to.'

The answer seemed trivial in comparison with Maria's troubled face.

'It's not possible.'

Bonaria stood up with a sigh. She had always known that this moment would come, but she had never for a moment imagined it would be like this.

'What's not possible? That he should have asked me or that I should have done it? You have eyes to see and you weren't born stupid, Maria. You knew Nicola and you know me.'

Maria shook her head violently.

'No, I don't know you. The person I know doesn't go into people's homes at night to suffocate cripples with pillows.'

The brutality of what she was saying clashed with the girl's whisper, slender as a tiny flame. As her suspicion gradually gained strength, the obscene implications of the truth multiplied in what she was saying.

'Does Giannina know? Does Salvatore Bastíu know?'

'It doesn't matter.' Bonaria knew she was lying but that did not stop her.

'The fact that his mother and father don't know that you killed their son doesn't matter?'

'That was how he wanted it, and I made him a promise.'

'Why on earth should Nicola have had to ask such a thing from you of all people?'

The old woman looked straight into Maria's face and said nothing. No words existed to answer that question, or if they did exist she did not know them. But in Maria's mind everything was suddenly clear and, in the instant she realized it, the daughter of Anna Teresa and Sisinnio Listru knew with certainty the truth about the woman standing before her. She opened her mouth to express her astonishment in a ritual oath, but all that came out was the gasp of a woman in childbirth, the sob of a strangled animal. She lifted her hand to her mouth, but held her eyes on the deathly pale face of the *accabadora*.

'All those times when you came back at night . . . ' she said.

'I would have told you when the right moment came, Maria.' Bonaria made no attempt to ease the girl's distress.

'When? When would you have told me? Would you have taken me with you? Would you have asked me to hold your shawl while you did it?' Anger grew on Maria's lips like a bitter foam. 'When would you have done that?'

'Not now, certainly. When you were ready for it.'

'Ready!' The word echoed in the room like an object flung to the floor. 'I would never have been ready to accept the idea that you killed people!'

As soon as it was clear that there was no damming the stream, Bonaria gave up all hope of finding a lighter or more gentle way of saying what had to be said.

'Don't start giving names to things you don't understand, Maria Listru. You will be faced by many choices you won't want to make in life, and you too, like the rest of us, will make them because they have to be made.'

'So this was one of those choices.' Maria's scorn was ferocious, and she made no attempt to hide the fact. 'And how do you go about doing this necessary thing? Why not tell me all about it, now you've got round to mentioning it?' She started walking round the table with a jerky step. 'Do you always go in secretly like you did with Nicola? No, let me think . . . or does the family call you, like the night when Santino Littorra came?' The more clearly she remembered it, the sharper the girl's anger seemed to become. 'And how do you do it, Tzia? Tell me that!'

Bonaria Urrai had seen enough of the world to know that rising to this provocation would not help.

'So you want to make decisions about the how without understanding the why? You're always in such a hurry to judge other people, Maria.'

'It's not me who's in a hurry, rather the opposite. If things have to happen, they will

156

happen of themselves when the right time comes.'

The old woman tore off her shawl and dropped it roughly on the chair. Her dark eyes fixed Maria with a certain impatient severity. Whatever the truth about Nicola, Bonaria Urrai was still capable of defending herself.

'They do happen of themselves,' she said with a cheerless smile. 'Do you think you were self-generated, Maria? Did you deliver yourself from your mother's belly by your own efforts? Or did you need help from someone else, like all living creatures?'

'I have always . . .' Maria said, but Bonaria stopped her with an imperious wave of the hand.

'Be quiet, you don't know what you're talking about. Did you cut the umbilical cord yourself? Didn't others wash you and breast-feed you? Were you not born and brought up twice, thanks to other people, or are you so clever that you were able to do it all by yourself?'

Recalled to her dependent status by what seemed to her an unfair blow beneath the belt, Maria stopped arguing, while Bonaria lowered her voice to a litany deprived of all emphasis.

'So others made decisions for you, and will

make more decisions when necessary. No-one alive has ever reached the light of day without the help of fathers and mothers at every corner of the road, Maria, and you more than anyone should know that.'

The elderly seamstress was speaking with the sincerity of a woman confiding in unknown fellow-travellers on a train, knowing she will never have to see them again.

'My own belly was never opened,' she said, 'and God knows whether I would have wished it, but I taught myself that children must be smacked and caressed, and be given the breast, and wine at festivals, and everything necessary at the time it is needed. I too had a part to play, and I have played it.'

'And what part was that?'

'The final part. I have been the last mother some people have seen.'

Maria stayed silent for a few minutes, her anger dying under the significance of those words, so unacceptable to her. When she did speak again, Bonaria knew there was nothing left for her to understand.

Maria said, 'You have been the most important person in my life, and if you asked me for death, I could not kill you just because you wanted it.'

Bonaria Urrai stared at her, and Maria saw that she was tired.

'Never say: I shall not drink from this water. You could find yourself in the water without having any idea how you got there.' Bonaria picked up the shawl she had dropped on the chair and slowly began to fold it, aware this was the only thing she still had the power to tidy away.

'That moment will never come.' Maria did not realize she had reached a decision until the moment it escaped her lips. 'I want to go away from you.'

If these words surprised the old woman, she did nothing to show it. She never even looked at the girl.

'I understand.'

'At once. Tomorrow.'

'Alright. I'll speak to your mother.'

'No.' The girl seemed to hesitate. 'I don't want to go back to my mother. I'll think of something else.'

'As you like.' This was not what Bonaria wanted to say, but she had been doing so many things she had not wanted to do in the last few days.

'Of course, I shall never forget the gratitude I owe you,' Maria added in a whisper.

The old woman looked at her, then said quietly:

'There is nothing I need that you can do

for me, Maria Listru.'

They went to bed without saying anything more because no more words were needed, but neither slept. The water in the pan on the spent hob was not the only thing that stayed cold that night in the former home of Taniei Urrai.

★   ★   ★

Early the next morning, Maestra Luciana opened the door to Maria, believing she had come to return the book she had borrowed; instead Maria had a suitcase in her hand and no meaningful explanation for it. But thirty years as a teacher had taught her that there are times for not asking questions, and before the end of the week Maria had a ticket for the Genoa ferry and an address in Turin on via della Tocca, where a family of the name of Gentili were waiting impatiently for the new Sardinian nanny specially recommended to them by Luciana Tellani.

14

A new life, that's what Maestra Luciana had told her. What you need is a new life, where no-one knows who you are, or whose daughter or what sort of daughter. Maria had not explained what had happened, or told her what she and Bonaria had said to each other, but one shrewd glance from the green eyes of the woman from Turin had been enough to make it clear to Maria that she herself was the only person in Soreni who had not known who Bonaria Urrai really was. She tried in vain to overcome the emptiness caused in her by this betrayal, which seemed to her so nearly a death, but without the consolation of being able to keep vigil beside the body of a loved person, or fencing round with earth in burial the tears that were suffocating her. She had lived for years with Bonaria in the belief that her double birth had made her equal to others, a right birth after a wrong one, but now the balance seemed a mass of errors and cancellations, leaving her out again like a left-over remainder.

A new life, Luciana Tellani had repeated firmly, as if being born again were simple. Yet she came to see that these were merely appropriate words, the sort that teachers reserve for eventualities like these, and the opportunity to establish at least one of her inconvenient multiplicity of births was a more powerful incentive than any other in persuading Maria to leave in such haste.

As she clung to the salty, sticky rail of the *Tirrenia* between Olbia and Genoa, she began to feel grown up and strong, almost free, without the shadowed eyes that so often become permanent in those forced to emigrate in search of food, people in no way looking forward to being born again in a new place. But Maria, as she cut the umbilical cord at a precise moment chosen by herself, remembered that day so long ago when, under the lemon tree in the yard of Anna Teresa Listru, she had first made up her mind what she wanted to put into her mud tarts. During the voyage Maria made a point of not sleeping at all, even for an hour. She needed every minute to process her memories as if she were herself an *accabadora*, judging the events of her life as if they were themselves people who might or might not be allowed to accompany her to the continent. She marked them off one by one, and by the time they reached Genoa she was convinced a burden had been lifted from her, and that she had left the whole dead weight of her wounds behind in the other land.

★   ★   ★

The walls of the home of Attilio and Marta Gentili, on the fifth floor of an expensive apartment block in the historic centre of Turin, were painted a creamy white that had nothing in common with the gaudy colours of homes in Soreni. Maria had only ever seen such white walls at school and at the hospital, and this too contributed to her sense of subjection, a subtle discomfort given added force by the ease with which they immediately addressed her with the familiar *tu*. The living-room Signora Gentili showed her into before going to call her children was a masterpiece of spaciousness, dominated by a large smoke-grey glass chandelier whose highly polished rounded drops hung from the ceiling like a great cluster of sucked sweets. In the few minutes she was left on her own, Maria stopped pretending not to be impressed by the high ceilings and the large art nouveau windows that occupied an entire wall; even at four in the afternoon with the sun already long past its zenith, she could imagine how the light must explode in there every cloudless morning. Trying to look at ease, she perched on the edge of the cream-coloured sofa, though she was in fact paralysed by the ostentation of so much unjustified space, which the little marble fireplace near the door certainly could not have been enough to heat; but it was a relief to be able to get to her feet when the Gentili children were brought in, though she was utterly unaware that, with her slender figure and bottle-green overcoat, she must seem to the children like nothing more than a rip in the wallpaper. With a certain solemnity Piergiorgio and Anna Gloria advanced hand-in-hand in front of their mother, dressed as if to create the illusion that they were twins. Maria offered an attempt at a smile, but Piergiorgio, already aware of the difference between reality and pretence, confined himself to staring at her from the awkward pride of his fifteen years, still firmly grasping his little sister's hand.

'Children, this is Maria.'

The wide flourish of the hand with which the signora indicated her to the children secretly annoyed Maria as it made her feel as if she had been acquired as part of the furnishings, but when she saw that Marta Gentili took the same attitude to her own children, she realized that it was just the mother's personal vision of the world.

'And these are my children, dear. Don't let their angelic air fool you, they are real earthquakes. Especially Piergiorgio!'

Maria smiled politely, even though she could not really see anything angelic in them. They were certainly good-looking, both with that uncertain fairness that tends to darken with age, but while Anna Gloria had inherited her mother's china-doll skin, Piergiorgio had the bronzed complexion of a ship's boy at sea, though this suggestion of warmth went no further than the rims of his cold blue eyes. Both had the hauteur of those born to wealth; it almost seemed they had long ago left the fragility and weaknesses of infancy behind them. But the white knuckles of their clenched fists would have revealed to a perceptive eye that all was not quite as it seemed. Maria instinctively understood as she studied them that her work would not be as easy as she had been led to believe, but that it might in the long run prove more interesting.

★ ★ ★

In accordance with the terms of her employment, Maria stayed with the children all the time they were not at school, following them in their games and duties regardless of whether their parents were at home or not.

165

She slept in the yellow room, a small space between the two larger ones reserved for the children, and the fact that it communicated with both led her to believe that it had probably been intended as a sort of large wardrobe area where eventually, when there was no more need for a nanny, both brother and sister would be able to store their clothes.

The first thing she had to reckon with was that they never went out to play with other children. It was true that the Gentili apartment had no access to a courtyard, but the street where they lived was very close to the large Valentino park and shady avenues along the Po, an exciting place where a mass of potentially fatal temptations would have driven any child mad with delight. But on this subject Marta Gentili was firm: the children could only be allowed outside with herself and their father. Going out to play without their parents was not even an option, and Maria very soon realized that part of her job was precisely to ensure that this never happened. In practice it was not a difficult rule to obey because Piergiorgio never showed any sign of wanting to go out and Anna Gloria, though more restless, seemed for the moment satisfied with her many fine toys. On the other hand Maria, in her few free hours, went out alone into the streets whenever she could, cautious but fascinated by the great city. Signora Gentili had told her the strange story of the rectangular street plan of Turin which seemed to have been designed in advance to fit the areas the streets were intended to lead to, on the principle that the citizens had had first to decide where they wanted to go, and only then to start planning and building their houses, squares and apartment blocks; the apparent illogicality of this led Maria to describe it in her first letters home to her sisters as an amusing novelty. This planning down to the last millimetre offended her good sense, convinced as she was that the only meaningful way to plan streets was the way it was in Soreni, where they seemed to have emerged from the houses like a seamstress's discarded scraps, clippings, and misshapen remnants, taken piecemeal from the spaces accidentally left over after the irregular emergence of the houses, which seemed to prop one another up like elderly drunks after a party given by their patron. Marta Gentili explained to Maria that the real reason for the geometrical plan of the streets of Turin had been security, since a royal capital must not offer rebels or enemies convenient places to hide, but this merely reinforced her view that to construct anything so deliberately on the basis of straight lines could only be an admission of weakness: who would ever take the trouble to design such straight streets unless they were trembling with fear?

All the same, she enjoyed walking aimlessly along the elegant arcades, looking into shop windows full of chocolate confectionery, or ready-made clothes draped with calculated formality round tailors' dummies. She would stop in front of the clothes shops and study them with her critical seamstress's eye, searching out badly made hems and uneven lapels and smiling with satisfaction when she detected such defects behind the shop windows. At moments like this she would think of Bonaria Urrai, but otherwise put all her strength into the delicate surgical operation she had started on the ferry, of which these walks were a fundamental part. The one thing she could not get used to was the insane cold of Turin; it was not just that it was cold — she had experienced that before — but the air was so frozen that to survive it she had to inhale in quick little snatches. The cold seriously threatened to spoil her pleasure, since it only took a few minutes to penetrate her thin coat, sticking knives even into her bones, despite her determinedly energetic walk.

The first times Maria came home with her

muscles tense and her stomach shrunk, it took her at least an hour to recover from the headache gripping her brow like a noose. She could not understand how the people of Turin could survive, but she was determined not to give in without a fight. The third time she came back numb with cold, she decided she must find a solution. With Marta Gentili's permission, she fished out of the newspaper basket in the living-room the daily papers which the master of the house had already read, and hid in her room to pin them on round her chest, back and stomach before putting on the green coat and venturing out into the street again. The cold seemed to find it more difficult to penetrate the smothered rustling of newsprint, and she kept her little secret all through the winter assisted by her convenient solitude: if she had had another girl to share her walks and sit with in cafés, it could have been complicated trying to explain, because she liked to keep her coat on as if glued to her while drinking her hot chocolate. But Maria had been careful not to make any friends. Meanwhile Attilio Gentili found it rather gratifying that his childrens' nanny seemed to be a passionate student of current affairs.

* * *

Looking after Anna Gloria proved less difficult than Maria had first feared, perhaps because, with her instinctive understanding of other natures as diffident as her own, she never made the mistake of trying to win her over with flattery, which the girl must have been only too accustomed to. What overcame Anna Gloria's instinctive shyness was the curiosity and passion that the little girl, bored by the amusements constantly thrust upon her, showed for tongue-twisters and word games, a speciality of Maria's. Together in the living-room they would laugh at comic pronunciations, while Maria would lift the child's fingers one by one as she recited her favourite rhyme:

'*Custu est su procu, custu dd'at mottu, custu dd'at cottu, custu si dd'at pappau et custu . . . ,*' here she would agitate her little finger wildly, making the little girl laugh fit to burst, ' *. . . mischineddu! No ndi nd'est abarrau!*'

'I understand nothing!' Anna Gloria would protest when she got over laughing at the strange-sounding words.

'That's just because you've never seen what can happen to a piglet in a family with four children.'

'Well, what can happen to a piglet in a family with four children?' the child would say, holding out her fist ready to start the game again.

Maria took the child's hand again with a conspiratorial air and started opening her fingers in order, beginning with her thumb.

'This is the pig, now he's dead, now he's cooked, and now . . . ' shaking the child's little finger like a bell, ' . . . poor little thing! There's nothing left of him!'

Maria taught her many other rhymes, some in Italian and some in Sard, and the child often unexpectedly repeated them with an ability that astonished her parents, to whom that simple glimmer of discipline seemed miraculous. Thanks to this ploy, after three weeks of tongue-twisting she and Anna Gloria were able to consider themselves, if not quite friends, at least accomplices, which enabled Maria to exercise at least a modicum of control over the rebellious and spoilt character of the little girl.

Piergiorgio Gentili was a quite different kettle of fish. From the very first he gave Maria no chance to establish any degree of familiarity, and though never less than polite, he seemed to Maria to aim every word or gesture precisely at ensuring a hostile distance between them. He noted with ill-concealed irritation the intimacies his little sister was sharing with the Sardinian girl and, while the two were enjoying themselves together, he would sit on the other side of the room, wary of the potential contagion of this new bond. Elegant by nature and very tall for his fifteen years, Piergiorgio had none of the comic adolescent awkwardness Maria had known in Andría Bastíu. Despite the clear signs of incipient manhood struggling furiously with the remnants of his childhood for control of him, there was something already decisive in the boy's dark look that disconcerted her and made her cautious of him.

Eventually the day came when Maria was able to learn what was hidden behind this behaviour. It was autumn in Turin, Piergiorgio was now sixteen and his sister eleven, and Maria had been working in the Gentili home for a year and ten months, during which time she had always lied to her sisters, writing that she was happy, that everyone treated her like a daughter and that she did not want to come home. From time to time Regina would pass on indirectly some item of news about Bonaria, who seemed to be suffering the natural infirmities of old age, but Maria systematically skipped anything that referred to the old seamstress.

'Why don't we go to the Valentino? It's a nice day.'

With that mock-natural statement, Anna

Gloria disturbed her brother's concentration on his Latin translation, while Maria lifted her head in astonishment from the braid she was using to edge a skirt. Attilio and Marta Gentili had gone as they often did to the Langhe dai Remotti, and would not be back before the next day.

'No.' Piergiorgio's tone of voice allowed no hint of explanation.

'Why not? We never go out, we're always at home, and we even go to school by car. We never go out for a walk, and I'm bored to death.' Anna Gloria turned to Maria, in the hope of support. 'What do you say?'

Piergiorgio looked hard at Maria for a moment, as if to discourage her from answering, then said:

'Since when has Maria been making the decisions?'

'Well, who does make the decisions then, you?' His sister challenged him, obstinate.

'Mamma and Papa make the decisions, and you know perfectly well they don't want us to go there.'

'They didn't when we were little, but we're big now. Anyway, we have Maria with us.'

Anna Gloria seemed in no mood to give in; she must have been planning her move for days, and Piergiorgio must in some way have realized it, because he got to his feet and in three strides covered the distance to his sister.

'You are still little and I don't want to go out. So we're staying at home. I think that's quite clear.'

The little girl was quiet, meeting the force of those eyes so similar to her own without allowing herself to be intimidated. Her impotence was driving her mad, but she kept her mouth shut.

'Good,' Piergiorgio said, satisfied with her silence.

After this, evidently intended as the end of the conversation, Piergiorgio went back to his desk, without letting anything in his attitude or look include Maria even by accident. Anna Gloria leaped to her feet, deliberately letting her geography book fall to the floor. Giving Maria a resentful look, she walked quickly out of the room, slamming the door behind her with a sharp sound that shook the coloured wooden clock on the wall. As though deaf, Piergiorgio kept his eyes firmly on his Latin exercise book. A few minutes later he and Maria could hear water running in the shower. Maria paid no attention; she was used to the explosive quarrels between the two that tended to pass as quickly as they started, but which were growing more frequent as Anna Gloria got older, and her rebellious nature became less and less inclined to tolerate the hitherto unchallenged authority of her brother. Piergiorgio pretended to be indifferent to these quarrels, but by now Maria knew enough to understand that in fact he knew no way to bridge the distance between himself and his sister. She kept this secret knowledge to herself, fully aware that this reciprocal game of pretences was the closest thing to complicity they would ever be able to share. But when after twenty minutes the water was still running in the shower, Piergiorgio raised his head from his books, and looked at Maria with an interrogative air.

'This shower's taking a long time.'

Maria broke off the knotted thread of her work, put the skirt down on the bed and went to look. Knocking on the bathroom door and getting no response, she opened it to find water pouring down from an empty shower. It took her only a few seconds to realize that Anna Gloria had never been under it at all.

'She's not here!' she said.

Returning to the room in alarm, she found Piergiorgio hastily pulling on his overcoat. He took the house keys from the cupboard and set off without worrying in the least whether anyone else was with him.

15

They ran down the stairs at breakneck speed, he agile as a cat, she following as fast as she could with her open coat flying behind her, anxious not to be left behind. It only took Piergiorgio an instant to realize that Anna Gloria was not in the road, before he started to run like a madman towards the Valentino park. Maria followed with her heart beating madly, more alarmed by his anxiety than by Anna Gloria's furtive escape. She had expected Anna Gloria's rebellious act; given her behaviour it was only a matter of time. What had taken her by surprise was the extreme reaction of her brother. She ran as fast as she could beside him, not so much in the hope of finding Anna Gloria — she was certain of that — but in the hope of reaching her at more or less the same moment as the desperate Piergiorgio.

They searched all over the park, but there was no trace of Anna Gloria. Running and stopping, searching the smaller paths with their eyes and hurrying quickly down the central one, after two hours Maria and Piergiorgio were out of breath but still side by side, he with a look of pure terror in his eyes, she much less optimistic than before about the outcome of their search. Breaking the silence imposed by breathlessness and reserve, they instinctively began to call her.

'Anna Gloria!' Maria shrieked.

'Anna!' Piergiorgio echoed in a strangled voice. Many turned to stare at the young woman and the boy with alarm and curiosity, but no-one answered their cries.

* * *

It was already six in the evening and the sun was setting when they came out of the park, perspiring and looking at one another in distress.

'It's your fault,' Piergiorgio said with hatred.

Maria winced but did not accuse him of injustice, because she knew perfectly well it was true: whatever had happened would in any case have been her fault. But she met his gaze, realizing that at the moment apportioning guilt was not the top priority.

'Let's try the river,' she said, trying to control her anguish.

They walked homewards, carefully following the water's edge, still calling out Anna Gloria's name but keeping their eyes fixed on the slope of the bank, terrified of seeing that someone had fallen in, of seeing something floating, or a motionless body among the trees near the water, from which a light haze was rising and making their search more difficult. They found nothing, but felt none the better for that and returned to via della Rocca full of anxiety, secretly hoping Anna Gloria might have got there before them.

The girl was indeed sitting waiting for them on the steps of the building, visibly nervous but clearly without the slightest intention of apologizing for her caprice. Piergiorgio stopped in the middle of the road, and Maria was worried by the flash she detected deep in his blue eyes. Presumably his sister was unaware of any danger, since she got to her feet and said:

'Well, here you are. I've been waiting out here at least an hour! Why on earth did you go off like that?'

For a few moments they both stared at her in disbelief. Maria was about to answer in the same tone, but Piergiorgio was too quick for her and his conciliatory words disturbed Maria more than if he had shouted.

'We felt like taking a walk. Since when do I have to account to you for what I do?'

Without waiting for an answer, he climbed the front steps with deliberate nonchalance, pulled the keys out of his pocket, and smoothly unlocked the front door of the building. Then he held it open for the other two to go in. Passing close to him, Maria saw an expression on his face she could not remember ever having seen before; for once, he was as pale as his sister. He gave Maria a warning look and, in accordance with this tacit pact, both behaved until evening as though nothing had happened. Anna Gloria for her part took good care not to press the argument, deceived by the silence into thinking that she had succeeded with her display of willpower in weakening the hold of the prohibition that had so weighed her down.

Of course, things were not so simple, though something must have snapped in Piergiorgio, because during the night Maria could hear from her room the unmistakable sound of barely suppressed weeping. Anna Gloria had often slipped into Maria's bed in her pyjamas to dispel the ghosts of a nightmare, or to share the sort of intimate confidences that can be made only in darkness, but in nearly two years the door separating her from Piergiorgio had never once been opened. Neither had seen it as real; for all it had to do with them, it might just as well have been merely a door drawn on the wallpaper. But faced with the sound of that weeping, there was no good reason for Maria not to breach the invisible barrier between them; the tension accumulated during the day had certainly made the rules seem both obscure and ineffectual, transformed by what had occurred into a limbo of temporary suspension.

When Piergiorgio noticed the door was open, his sobbing stopped abruptly. His voice, broken but harsh, rose from the utter darkness of the room.

'What do you want?'

'I could hear you.'

'So? Go away.'

'No.'

'I said go away. This is not your room.'

Moving forward in the darkness, Maria had no fear of tripping over anything; she knew the maniacal order in which the boy kept his things. Suddenly the bedside table lamp came on, showing Piergiorgio fully dressed on his bed, sitting with his back against the headboard and his pillow pressed between his knees, marked with the wet bites where he had been trying to hide his weeping. His face was red like that of a small child, but there was nothing childish about his rigid jaw and furious glare.

'Let's talk.'

'What about?'

'You know. About what happened today.'

'I've nothing to say to you. Anyway, nothing happened.'

He was looking at Maria with the same ferocious hatred she had seen when he accused her in the park.

'Please forgive me,' she said.

Seeing her give in without a fight he seemed to waver, but his hands were still clutching the pillow like a shield.

'What are you asking to be excused for?' he asked.

'I don't know,' Maria said, which was the truth. 'What are you accusing me of?'

Piergiorgio hesitated; he had never liked straight questions. Maria could clearly see the telltale up-and-down movement of his Adam's apple, giving him away.

After a short pause he echoed her words: 'I don't know.' But his eyes were still passing judgement.

She moved further into the room, disarmed and disarming in her yellow flannel pyjamas, asking everything she wanted to ask at once as if afraid she would never have another opportunity to hear the answers.

'Then why do you always treat me as if there's something about me that needs excusing? Where have I gone wrong? What have I done to you?'

Piergiorgio silently watched her come nearer the bed. Then he said stiffly,

'You've done nothing. It wasn't you, it was her.'

'Exactly, it has nothing to do with me.'

Suddenly, Maria sat down on the edge of the bed, deliberately invading the space that, huddled in one corner, he was guarding with his eyes. She had never been a cautious person, but never as reckless as at that moment, in which she sensed a fleeting mystery she felt it would have been irresponsible to ignore. She made no effort to calculate the risks of seizing the moment as she stared in silence into his blue eyes, seeing them change in character, assuming an empty, lost expression, dangerously absent. When he reached for the light-switch, Maria did nothing to stop him, and the sudden darkness took away the breath of both, just as much as the course of events that afternoon had done.

For a few seconds Piergiorgio said and did nothing, then he started to speak. At first he whispered, seeming to return to a conversation that had been interrupted, but which in reality had never even started. At first Maria did not understand why he was telling her a story of hide-and-seek and small children's races, but then his words began to explode in the darkness with revelations almost as painful for her to listen to as they must have been for him to make. She was not at all certain he was speaking to her; rather she had the impression that he had turned the light off to be able to forget that she was there at all, and this understanding stopped her saying a single word.

In the darkness she could see him as a small child, his hair fairer than now, playing hide-and-seek with other children under the careless eye of the first nanny employed to look after him. As he recalled the past, Piergiorgio's voice gradually lost its power until it was as light as the voice of the little boy hiding among the trees by the river while he waited heart in mouth as his friends struggled to find him, before dashing like a rat for the agreed tree, shouting at the top of his voice 'Home! I'm the quickest!' He had always been good at hiding; even at home his father and mother had to search for him for ages when he did not want to be found. But on this particular occasion his friends had problems finding him because it was difficult to see through the bushes on the riverbank, and even more difficult for them to reach him on their short legs. But for the vigilant eyes of an adult who had time to wait, and for the strong legs of an adult who knew how to search and find, that cunning hiding-place on the riverbank would have been perfect for playing hide-and-seek with a child. Piergiorgio did not yet know that grown-ups do not play hide-and-seek in the bushes with children.

While the nanny was chattering with the other girls paid to look after other people's children, and while the other children were playing hide-and-seek as best they could with the setting sun flattening the trees against the ground in mobile, fugitive shadows, Piergiorgio Gentili got lost in the bushes and fell into the hands of a stranger, and no-one ever reported or even discovered the fact. The child they did find many hours later by the river had become incapable of hiding, or of throwing his arms round anyone at all, or ever trusting anyone again, and his parents thought he must have fallen, probably slipping on the bank, and that a blow to his head had perhaps knocked him out until sunset, or perhaps he had suffered the fear of death that all children experience when they pretend to hide and get lost and no-one comes to find them. Marta Gentili sacked the nanny on the spot and Piergiorgio equally abruptly even forgot her name, and from that moment neither he nor his sister were allowed ever again to play in the park or along the riverbank or anywhere else. Piergiorgio never told either his father or mother that everything they dreaded happening had already happened, and for ten years he had never said anything at all about it until that night, when he told the whole story to Maria in the darkness of his room, with his shoulders pressed against the bedhead and his head buried in a bush on the riverbank, remembering the smell of mud and other people's sweat.

Maria could not have said at what precise stage of the horror that Piergiorgio was describing she had moved closer without interrupting him, or at what precise point she had taken him in her arms, nor would he have been able to name the moment when he had begun in the darkness to let shamed tears fall silently from his eyes. Morning surprised them in a blameless sleep, locked in an embrace in which he had finally found himself again, and she had lost herself.

From that moment Piergiorgio's attitude to Maria changed completely. He became courteous and almost considerate. He no longer answered her in monosyllables, and, in fact, even spoke to her when she had not spoken first; he helped her to carry clothes she had been ironing, offered to open doors for her when her arms were full of shopping, and at table was quick to pass everything before she asked for it, to the astonishment of the rest of the family. This gallantry was a particularly pleasant surprise to Attilio Gentili who, in the first clear fires of his son's adolescence, detected promising signs of a precocious maturity. On the other hand, this incomprehensible change in Piergiorgio made his mother suspicious, and particularly annoyed Anna Gloria who, aware of the effect Maria was having on him, found herself suffering a jealousy she had never before experienced. As soon as she realized that something had changed, the complicity she had built up with the Sardinian girl vanished overnight, and the more considerately her brother treated Maria, the more impatient his sister became at the idea of her remaining as their nanny. Maria for her part cared nothing about Anna Gloria's attitude, but seemed to have developed a sort of protectiveness towards Piergiorgio that had no reason to exist, since the boy was now well past the age of needing anyone to look after him; especially since Maria had never really fulfilled this role, as they both knew.

It was now that Maria for the first time began to be aware of the budding manhood of his body as the softness of childhood disappeared from the ever more marked features of his face, and as his shoulders grew broader daily, emphasizing a natural grace that till then had merely seemed out of focus. The door between the two bedrooms was no longer just a picture on the wall, and the nights were filled with murmurs and laughter, carefully but happily smothered by the perpetrators, perfectly aware that what they were doing could not, ultimately, be considered innocent. They had nothing to hide, yet both made every effort to hide it. What they could not hide was visible in the mornings at breakfast, when the two insomniacs could not conceal the dark shadows under their eyes from the boy's unobservant parents but more particularly from the surly searching gaze of Anna Gloria as she rhythmically chewed toast, tense with increasing fury. Maria no longer went out as much, and when she did, she no longer fastened newspapers under her coat; she was in the grip of a burning fever that, had it not blinded her, she would have recognized. It was not the first time such a fever had coursed through her veins, but previously she had only been aware of it as the backwash after a wave, and this time it would be no different.

In Piergiorgio's adoring eyes she saw herself as beautiful in a way she could not remember ever having felt before, as beautiful as when she wore the bread crown on her head in her mother's fragrant bedroom and had seen herself reflected in the wardrobe mirror, with her bare breast and the little gold chain that had given her the distinction of a lady in a portrait. Her sister's husband had certainly never seen her like this, and even Andría Bastíu's love for her had been more homely: they had never shared in the confession of secrets so foul as to stain the night for ever, nor had Maria ever been afraid to touch his hand for fear of making the blood surge under her skin, as constantly happened when she looked at Piergiorgio's fine profile. She had always known she was female, but only now did she discover what it felt like to be a woman, because no-one had ever before shown it to her with the passionate frenzy she saw in the eyes of the sixteen-year-old Piergiorgio Gentili every time he looked at her.

★   ★   ★

As the weeks passed, instinctively aware of the dangerous hostility of Anna Gloria, Maria and Piergiorgio became more furtive, carefully avoiding situations in which they themselves might bring an end to Maria's continued but now virtually superfluous presence in the house. At night they only met for a few minutes at a time, careful as thieves not to touch each other even accidentally, before returning to their own beds with the hot guilt of perpetually frustrated desire. Maria knew a mere gesture would have been enough to tip the balance, and she was extremely careful not to let this happen, bridging the distance between them with other little intimacies. It was as if both realized that their instinctive need for one another at the time of sleep made them a separate entity in the ecosystem of the house, an organism too fragile to risk exposing it to infection through an incautious exchange of fevers.

This care saved Maria in many ways, though at first she was not aware of it. She was too wrapped up in what was happening to realise that their mutual comings and goings at night were having an effect not only on Piergiorgio's wounded past, but also on her own. If he seemed to have succeeded in resolving certain memories, she was inadvertently beginning to awaken others, in a game of interrelationships that seemed to have no apparent logic. Many things that she thought she had left behind when the ferry sailed for Genoa now came back one after the other, like pieces of wood thrown up on the beach after a storm at sea.

The first time Maria realized that something was changing was one night, as she was slowly returning barefoot to her room. The feel of the moquette carpet under her feet suddenly brought back the shaggy tawny fur of Mosè, and the exact colour of the dog's round eyes. And so her first memories began to surface, always at night and when she was unexpectedly distracted by a physical sensation. Then memories began to surface by day too, when she could no longer blame the tricks of sleep if the angle of a sunbeam in the living-room reminded her of sunlight in the house of Bonaria Urrai. Slowly they came back to her one by one, faces, voices and places from her childhood, and Maria discovered that she could inhabit them effortlessly. While she was sewing, the slow rhythms of her hand would unconsciously echo other needlework, already experienced somewhere else, on different cloth but not in a different life, though she had been arguing the opposite with herself for months.

She never spoke about what was happening to her. She was convinced that these capricious scraps of memory which others would have dismissed as sudden homesickness were not something she could reveal to Piergiorgio. But meanwhile present and past faced one another as if after an armistice, burdening her breast with the dumb gratitude of survivors. She had long ago stopped stealing little things that already belonged to her, but now once again she found she had something to hide, since the awareness she shared with Piergiorgio was not and never could be true reciprocity. Her self-denial contained a bitter prophecy, and Maria knew she was the only one who could be aware of this. The fear of seeing it proved true forced her to move round the boy's soul like someone walking on sand, afraid to leave too many traces of her footsteps. Every time he passionately sought to invoke eternity or other inconvenient guests on their behalf, Maria understood better that what divided them was not age or social status, so much as the persistence in him of the childish self-deception of confusing what one wants with what one has. This was why, every time she left his room and closed the door behind her after their final whisper, Maria renewed to herself her rejection of the man Piergiorgio would become.

★ ★ ★

The obvious fact that she could never be more than a temporary presence in the Gentili home did not prevent her from feeling that the ground was opening under her feet when a letter arrived from Regina asking her to come home at once. Just a few lines: her sister was good at many things but writing was not one of them. She had put down just the necessary minimum, and after she had opened the letter Maria kept it on her bedside table for two days, pretending it had not even arrived.

It was not until the third night that she found the courage to go into Piergiorgio's room to tell him how things stood, and the anxiety of imminent loss was so great as to make her forget her caution. She did not wait to be sure that Anna Gloria was asleep before opening the door, and the slight squeak of the handle was enough to give the other girl the signal she had long been hoping for. While in the darkness Maria was sustaining the weight of Piergiorgio's fury on being faced with the necessity of her decision, the light in the bedroom was suddenly switched on from outside, revealing the two young people in confusion in each other's arms on the bed, but this was more than enough for the astonished eyes of Attilio and Marta Gentili. Piergiorgio and Maria did not protest their innocence, and they were undoubtedly not innocent, but they kept to themselves the precise nature of their fault, according to a pact that had never needed to be other than unspoken. The next day Anna Gloria shed not a single tear as Maria, overcome with shame, went down the stairs with her suitcase. Piergiorgio had not even been allowed to leave his room to say goodbye, and the money due to her was coldly handed over without references by the head of the family in an envelope that she did not even open for many days; the only envelope she repeatedly opened to reread its contents was the one from her sister Regina, which in a single alarming sentence added to the pain of parting the weight of responsibility likely to face her on arrival: 'Mariedda darling, come back at once if you can: Bonaria Urrai has had a stroke and may be dying.'

16

The table-lamp had been turned off, but Bonaria Urrai did not need the light to know that Maria was sitting there somewhere in the shadows of the hospital room. It was not easy to say exactly when she had developed the habit of sitting to look at Bonaria in silence in the dark, whether she had always had this habit or whether she had developed it on the continent, in the place where she had been working and which she had not wanted to talk about to Bonaria. Bonaria suspected that Maria had picked up the nasty habit of spying on people in their sleep from herself, and she would have liked to have yielded to the temptation to tell Maria she was aware of it, perhaps starting with some sort of noise to make it clear from the first that she was awake. But something stopped her and she did not do it, just as she had not done it at the very beginning, before time decided to escape from her hand like a wolf in the night.

★ ★ ★

At the very beginning.

It had been silent in the shop, and Bonaria could still remember Anna Teresa Listru with her plaited hair dipping her stumpy hands into the bag of white beans from Tonara, as if to pick them out one by one. She had been eagerly sharing some gossip with the shopkeeper and the pharmacist's wife, a woman from the continent, who was wearing a dark fur like a city lady as she carefully examined the various kinds of soup on display behind the glass windows of the showcase.

Amid those three women Maria had been as nothing, like an expiry date that has to be noted down so as not to be forgotten; she had not even benefited from the sort of nice things women usually say when they want to compliment other women on their children. Bonaria, sitting on a sack of dried beans in a corner, was waiting for the arrival of the daily milk delivery and watching the forgotten child moving about quickly among things of her own height: fruit, coloured plastic whirligigs, a large basket of fresh bread and her mother's rough knees.

The old woman's eyes were the only ones to notice a handful of black cherries secretly vanishing from a basket into a pocket among the folds of Maria's little white dress. Tzia

Bonaria saw neither shame nor self-awareness in the little girl's face, as if this absence of judgement was the just counterpoise to her invisibility. Faults, like people, only exist if there is someone to notice them. But Maria was moving innocently along the counter where the other women were discussing the increased price of vegetables, creeping like an insect through the narrow space between the bottoms of her mother and the pharmacist's wife, attracted by the latter's dark glossy fur. She was staring at it with her mouth half-open, bewitched by the reflections that shimmered over the fur at the woman's every movement. Bonaria Urrai knew what the little girl was about to do even before Maria's fingers reached out to commit that downy sin. The child immersed her hand in the dense pelt, never before seen on a Christian, amazed that death could be so soft. The pharmacist's wife showed no sign of having noticed anything, which encouraged Maria to go a little further. Moving close to that bum, grown fat on the ailments of others, she buried her face in the dark fur and avidly inhaled its smell. It was only then that the wife of the pharmacist became aware of this fingering of her person and let out a cry of annoyance, attracting everyone's attention to Maria.

Now, stretched out in bed, Bonaria Urrai managed a feeble smile in the darkness at the sudden recovery of this memory of Maria, of Maria made substantial and real in this individual sin of a solitary child. But Bonaria did not see her cry that morning in the shop, while her mother struggled to find words to explain her uncouth behaviour, a sensory deprivation that had driven her to theft much more often than could have been justified by hunger:

'I never wanted her, because God knows three children are plenty for a woman in my situation . . . '

Not even that retroactive abortion had provoked any reaction on Maria's face. She had stayed motionless with the numb unconsciousness of those who have never been properly born, while the colour of the stolen cherries began to spread over the white material from the right-hand pocket of her dress. A telltale redness spreading like a wound, almost black in some places. It was as if the stain was the only thing about her that was real, an obscene menarche of fruit. The shopkeeper was the first to see it.

'Have you been taking cherries from the basket?'

When Anna Teresa Listru became aware of the havoc on her daughter's dress the slap was already on its way. The child did not close her eyes until the instant the hand hit her, then opened them again with a steady gaze and one hand thrust fiercely into her pocket, aggravating the external stain. Her tears were there, but she hid them.

'Giulia, I'm so sorry, I don't know what to say, add them to my bill . . . '

'Don't worry, these things happen, they're just children.' Behind the counter the shop-keeper played it down. 'Though of course that mischievous hand . . . ' she added maliciously with a half-smile.

More than anything else, it was that red stain on the little embroidered pocket that had made it clear to Bonaria Urrai that the barren period of her life might be over, and less than a week later she had gone to talk to Anna Teresa Listru about the possibility of taking Maria as a soul-child. And she had added an offer that Sisinnio Listru's widow could not even dream of refusing. In any case Bonaria had devoted herself since her early years to dressmaking, because if she was really good at anything, it was taking the measure of people. And here too she made no mistake. Anna Teresa Listru accepted the plan without discussion, and ten days later Maria was already installed in her room in the ancestral home of the Urrai family, never

198

even having been told that a fundamental change in her family status was envisaged.

* * *

Even after so many years, Maria was not yet sure how far the course of her life had deviated from the one chosen for her. The only thing that had been in the agreement from the beginning was this bed, at which her attendance now had the weight of the completion of a bargain. Tired of pretending to believe Bonaria was sleeping, she approached her pillow and said:

'I know you're awake. Can I bring you anything?'

Bonaria opened wide her eyes, their pupils watered down by a veil of cataract, and saw Maria as nothing more than a vague shape. There was too little light in the room, and it had been kept like that for days, because the doctor had said strong light could give the patient a headache, as though Bonaria's problem was migraine. She would have burst out laughing if she had been capable of it, but the stroke had partly paralysed her face, preventing even such a simple movement. In order to smile, Doctor Sedda had told her, she needed dozens of muscles, and she had lost the use of nearly all of them.

'Water . . . ' she seemed to be saying.

Maria interpreted the mumbled vowels, and lifted the beaker with its straw to her mouth; the nurse had not yet come to insert the hydration drip in her arm. With a struggle Bonaria sucked water from the beaker, but her inability to control her lips sent some up her nose and some outside her mouth. She coughed violently, and Maria tried to lift her to make it easier for her to swallow the little water she had managed to get into her throat.

* * *

Bonaria had been in this state for nearly two months, and her age made it difficult for the doctors to predict any degree of recovery.

Maria's return to Sardinia had surprised no-one. 'It's right for a soul-child,' they said at Soreni, as if this were a destiny she could not escape. But in reality few had believed she would actually return to fulfil it. Noting her hasty departure from the village, some had even said she had gone away because she was pregnant by Andría Bastíu, since the two of them had been constantly together, and the fact that there was not the slightest evidence to support the idea was for some the ultimate proof that it must be so. But in any case, everyone believed that something must have happened between the two women to break the sacred pact of adoption, restoring them to their earlier status of undowered orphan and childless widow.

But Anna Teresa Listru's daughter had come back, and she seemed to have done so specially to pay her debt in the moment of need. In the eyes of the community, this restored to her the right of inheritance that she would not otherwise legally have been able to claim, and there was no harm in believing that she had done it for precisely this reason. From the point of view of inheritance, Maria could certainly call herself fortunate, though people did not assess her fortune so much on the volume of goods that would come to her as on the time she would have to spend looking after the old woman before the Lord decided she had eaten enough bread. There had been girls who had wasted the best years of their lives on tyrannical old women who could not make up their minds to die, with the irony of fate allowing them enormous inherited fortunes at an age when they no longer felt they could make the most of them. But this was not the case with Maria, since Bonaria Urrai was obviously more than halfway gone. She could not chew her food, and the paralysis of the right side of her body made it impossible for her to get out of bed and attend to her personal hygiene. Maria did everything for her with a dedication not even to be expected of a daughter, and on their doorsteps in the evening the old women praised the devotion of her self-sacrifice, ever more impressive the nearer it came to martyrdom.

In fact Maria, who made every effort to appear utterly serene in everything she did, was terrified by the idea that Bonaria might be dying, and the old woman knew her too well not to have realized it. They did not speak, and had not done so since Maria came back — in any case Bonaria still could not do so — but they had looked at one another often in the gloomy room, and had worked out between them a language that avoided most misunderstandings. The words spoken that evening when the Bastíu family had been mourning Nicola still lay between them, but it was clear that Maria was waiting, even if there was no hope that Bonaria would ever be able to speak in an articulate manner again.

When after four months it was finally clear that the condition of the old woman would never improve, she was discharged from hospital and the doctors allowed Maria to take her home, after explaining how to care for her in what was now agreed to be an unchanging state of health. What this meant was that Bonaria was stuck on the threshold of death, but at first Maria refused to accept this and treated her like a convalescent, with such dedication that after a few weeks Bonaria's control over the movement of her lips improved to such an extent that she was able to articulate simple words, and ask for what she needed. For her part, Bonaria Urrai felt there were things between them that needed saying, but that in all probability could never be said. The long protraction of Bonaria's state of immobility made it clear that she was one of those old people destined to die slowly, but while having time to reflect and beg pardon for his sins would have been a blessing for Don Frantziscu Pisu, it was certainly nothing of the sort for the *accabadora*. The old priest came to see her a couple of times to mumble over her paralysed body a series of short prayers in Latin which he only half knew how to pronounce. Bonaria, respecting his good intentions, let him go ahead, but after he had gone she made it clear to Maria that she would not welcome more visits from the priest.

With time even the visits of the curious became less frequent, until the only person left to look after Bonaria was Maria, helped from time to time by the expert hands of Giannina Bastíu. The old woman lost weight, but even so it was not at all easy to lift her from her bed, since her bones had become so fragile that there was a risk that even too vigorous a grasp might cause them to fracture.

★ ★ ★

Bonaria Urrai languished like this for nearly a year before entering her death throes without ever having said any of the words she had wanted to say to Maria. She remained lucid, though she could only speak with her eyes. But by now Maria did not even need a gesture to understand what Bonaria needed. She slept in the same room and got up several times each night to check that the old woman was still alive; as soon as she had the tiniest confirmation of this she would go back to her camp bed.

It was during one of those nights that Bonaria Urrai started shouting. She did not exactly cry out, but the moans emerging from her mouth had a note of violent desperation about them. Maria got out of bed, and understood at once that it was not water that Bonaria wanted. In recent weeks her suffering had become more intense, and her body had become so frail that even a simple massage could have been enough to crush her increasingly fragile bones. Though so far she had complained little, it now seemed that she could bear it no longer, and her wide-open eyes searched Maria's face with ravenous desperation. Maria found herself much weaker than she had always believed herself to be. The sounds the old woman was making drove her on the first night to leave the room so as not to have to listen to the rattle in her throat. But on the second night she forced herself to remain, doing her best to soothe her. But it was pointless, and the third night Maria stayed weeping on her camp bed. Bonaria could hear her clearly, and moaned so loudly that Maria thought she would die of exhaustion, in fact she almost wished she would, but in the morning the old woman was still painfully alive. After two weeks of this torture, the girl began to understand what Bonaria had meant three years earlier when she had said: 'Never say: I shall not drink from this water.'

17

Protection or guilt. At Soreni these were the only things that could cause a bad death, and Maria did not know which of the two was preventing Bonaria Urrai from taking her leave. In her uncertainty, she decided to deal with things over which she had some control. Just as Bonaria had done many years earlier for her, she cleared the shelves of images of the sacred heart and mystic lamb, and took away the holy-water stoup with its raised relief of Santa Rita. Next she took down all the religious pictures from the bedroom walls, removed images taken from the pages of books or hidden at the bottom of drawers, untied all green ribbons from doorhandles, and swept from the corners every piece of horn meant to guard against spirits. Most important of all, she carried away the blessed Holy Week palm hanging behind the door, completely dried out but not for this reason innocuous. The old woman was wearing no scapulars or other objects that might hold her back; only her baptismal chain, which Maria took off her neck with great care while Bonaria fixed her eyes on her without protest.

After this, they waited. For the next two weeks Bonaria, hardly more than skin and bone, continued to teeter on the edge of death without falling over it.

As the days passed, Maria decided in her utter impotence that what was forcing Bonaria Urrai to cling so agonizingly to life could not be protection. The same night she went to sit beside the old seamstress's bed, gazing at her in silence. After a few minutes Bonaria opened her veiled eyes and fixed her with a stare.

'What must I do?' Maria said.

The old woman seemed to be trying to say something, but all that came from her mouth was a struggling breath. Maria knelt down beside the bed with her elbows on the coverlet, aware of the ever stronger sour smell of the old woman. When she spoke it was with deliberate slowness:

'You are in penance for something you have done, Tzia.'

At these words Bonaria closed her eyes, in a simulation of sleep that Maria found entirely unconvincing. She took the old woman's hand.

'Who have you injured?'

The eyelids remained closed and the old woman's hand did not move. It occurred to Maria that even death could not have made her more absent.

'You are not allowed to go because you have debts, but only you know what they are. I can go from house to house asking forgiveness on your behalf, and when this is all over, I'll know I've found the right one.'

The old woman reacted to these words as if to a threat, opening wide her clouded eyes and fixing them on the face of her adopted daughter. Her hand contracted in a surprisingly strong spasm and Maria, not expecting such resistance, took it as confirmation, and continued:

'I'll start with the Bastíus.'

Bonaria Urrai emitted a groan like a shout. Determined to understand, Maria did not move from the bedside where she was kneeling.

'Don't you want that?'

The old woman barely moved her head, but her denial was very clear.

'Don't you understand that this is why you can't go in peace?'

Bonaria stared blankly at Maria with a stubborn determination but without any visible shadow of remorse. Confronted with that fierce willpower, their roles were for an instant reversed, and Maria felt that it was she who was paralysed. She gently withdrew her hand from the convulsive grip of the old woman.

For the next few days Maria acted as if this conversation had never happened, busying herself just as usual. She cleaned Bonaria, fed her and combed the few thin hairs left on her fragile skull, chatting to her about the weather and the scant local news, ignoring the fact that Bonaria had never taken any interest in such matters. The old woman suffered from cramps and other pains, especially at night, but no degree of suffering seemed able to put a final end to her strength. Bonaria Urrai continued to live, there were no two ways about it.

When the moment was right, Maria returned to the subject of their discussion, after carefully feeding Bonaria the last teaspoonful of her pear purée. Having no appetite, Bonaria had refused half of it, and Maria knew that within an hour at most she would deposit the other half on her bib, left in place for that reason.

'Have you thought about what I said to you?' she said, putting the plate on the bedside table.

The old woman did not pretend not to understand; rather her immobility constituted a clear assent.

'Tzia,' Maria said, coming closer to the bed, 'I can't bear to see you like this. If there was anything I could do . . . '

With a struggle Bonaria took hold of her hand, and squeezed it as hard as her weakness permitted. It was not a strong grip, but there was something spirited about it that affected Maria more than if she had been bitten. The old woman tried to articulate a word or two, and Maria bent to catch what she was trying to say. A light breath touched her cheek like a tentative caress, but there were no clear words. She searched for meaning in the old woman's eyes, but instantly regretted having wanted to understand. Bonaria Urrai was staring at her with such intensity that she had to turn away.

'Tell me what you'd like me to do,' she said in terror.

When it was clear there would be no answer, she left the bed and carried the plate to the kitchen with her heart beating like a hammer on hot iron.

The same evening she went to the Bastíu house to look for Andría. They had met once or twice since her return, but always with the guilt felt by victims of theft, incapable of reviving the confidence that had once made them accomplices in the unconfessable crimes for which children are capable of blaming themselves before being given to understand that they are innocent. Giannina occasionally came to help with Bonaria, but

Maria had not set foot in the Bastíu house since the day Nicola died.

Andría did not seem surprised to see her, and received her with a certain ill-concealed coolness. He was much taller than Maria remembered him, with a trace of piratical beard that gave him a look utterly incongruous with his kindly eyes, which were still just as Maria remembered them. This gave her the strength to tell him what she had come for, and when she had finished Andría stood up abruptly and stuck his hands into the pockets of his jeans.

'Did she ask you that?'

'She can't speak.'

'That's not an answer. Has she given you to understand that she would want me to do it?'

Maria hesitated, but she had no intention of lying.

'No, on the contrary.' Then she added at once: 'But I'm sure this is why she's still suffering.'

Andría shook his head vigorously, then gave her a serious look, clearly unwilling to see things from her point of view.

'It makes no sense, and you're behaving like a superstitious old woman. If she doesn't kick the bucket, it's because her time hasn't come.'

At these crude words Maria was overcome

by an irresistible wave of impatience, and got to her feet in her turn. They faced each other across the room like two caged dogs looking for a chance to sink their teeth into each other. But Maria was the weaker of the two, and she knew it.

'Maybe if she could look at you, if you could speak to her . . . Come and see her!'

He was aware of the note of real desperation in the girl's voice but he showed no sign of pity. When he answered, there was something so ferocious in his tone that Maria clearly saw the limitations of the platitude that time heals all suffering.

'The continent has done you no good, our Mariedda. You've become so arrogant about other people's sins. Has it never struck you that there may be nothing to forgive?'

Surprised and hurt, Maria returned his look, opening her mouth to speak. Then she shut it again without a word, and Andría went on.

'Because you seem so sure of your . . . But perhaps you're wrong, perhaps in heaven they don't judge people the way you do.'

'I thought you'd understand . . . he was your brother!'

'Of course he was my brother. And he wanted to die.'

They looked at each other, Maria's face

uncomprehending, Andría's tense and hard.

'You've changed too. That day you didn't talk like this.'

'We all grow up, Marí. Or did you assume you'd always be the clever one?'

The accomplice of her childhood games was lost; instead she was faced with a stranger intent on brutally revenging himself on her in more ways than one. Maria felt exhausted, and even worse, stupid.

'I should never have come. I don't even know now why I did, I'm sorry.'

She left without another word, and he did not even see her to the door, staying on the hard sofa in the front room, having chosen on purpose to meet her in the room for strangers, the room for tiresome visits and funeral vigils.

When Bonaria heard the front door open, the thought that Maria might not be alone sent coursing through her veins the little adrenalin her body was still capable of producing. But it closed again and the girl came in alone, with a defeated air. That evening Maria ate her supper alone by the fire before going into Bonaria's room to check the flow of the drip; when she replaced it by the weak light of the bedside lamp, the old woman gave no sign of having noticed. Then she went to her own room and wept all the rage and pain out of her body. She wept so much that she could no longer remember whether she was crying for the dying or for someone already dead.

*   *   *

A week later Bonaria Urrai fell into a coma. Doctor Mastinu said it would not be long now, and Maria did not feel like reminding him that he had said the same thing six months ago. Don Frantziscu asked whether he should come to administer extreme unction, and from the way Maria told him she would let him know in good time, he understood there would never be a convenient moment, but had enough shame to hide his relief.

Maria's life with the living corpse of Bonaria Urrai was a monotonous lament that no-one but she seemed able to hear. She continued as before, interpreting her waiting with the vision of an architect who must build houses before the roads that will lead to them exist. Despite Doctor Mastinu's words, three months later Bonaria Urrai was still imprisoned in her own body as if suspended on a thread of steel too slender to be visible but too strong to snap. And her adopted daughter shared her condition with her.

It was at the end of a day spent

embroidering sheets for some woman's wedding and raging solicitously around the old woman's inert body, that something in Maria wavered. The unthinkable assailed her while she was changing the pillowcase on the bed for a freshly laundered one. It was the very softness of the pillow that touched her, nothing more than that, but it might have been more than enough for that tiny stream of breath. The image was brief, but so intense that Maria was forced to sit down, horrified at her own daring. She let the pillow fall to the floor and stared at it as though it were a poisonous snake. From that moment she moved circumspectly round the bed, carefully watching her own movements, afraid of herself. The thought came to her again, always unexpectedly, sometimes when she was asleep, sometimes by day when she was busy with ordinary household duties, innocent actions concealing ferocious possibilities she had never even imagined. She began to dread being alone at night in Bonaria's room. In the weeks that followed, the idea of acting to end their mutual imprisonment gradually became less shocking: each time the thought came to her it seemed to be a little less sacrilegious and abrupt and more gentle and feasible.

In the Gentili home, during her nights spent talking to Piergiorgio, Maria had come to understand that many things that actually happen are merely parodies of things imagined; for this reason, once Bonaria had fallen into a coma, she was perfectly aware that she could have killed her countless times without anyone ever knowing, not even the doctor who still came regularly to monitor the state of this deathless decomposition. Then one morning in June when she thought she was opening the door to the doctor, she found herself facing the tall, sturdy figure of Andría Bastíu.

'*Ciao*,' he said, not coming in.

'*Ciao*.' She was too surprised to remember to show hostility.

'Can I come in?' She remembered her manners.

'Of course, sorry. Come in, it's just that . . . '

'You weren't expecting me,' he said calmly.

Maria took him into the kitchen, where he made straight for the place that always used to be his own, near to the fire where Mosè, no longer subject to Bonaria's prohibitions, was sleeping placidly. He stopped near the dog, but stayed standing.

'Sit down, I'll make you some coffee.' She pointed to the chair.

'Never mind coffee, that's not what I came for.'

'Why did you come, then?' She stared at him.

The surviving Bastíu son shifted slightly on the chair, then indicated the corridor.

'To see her.'

The words made Maria smile with a sort of bitter grimace that momentarily distorted her face.

'Now you want to see her . . . '

Andría's anger seemed to have vanished, as if he had poured it all out that evening before Christmas, when she had been the one to beg him to come. She nodded with a weary sigh, and he followed her slowly down the corridor, keeping pace with her. The bedroom was still dimly lit, despite the fact that Bonaria no longer noticed either light or darkness. The body, reduced to its basic functions, was so tiny that the bed seemed about to swallow it up in its covers. Andría stopped a moment at the door and looked to Maria for a sign, then went to Bonaria's bedside. Maria did nothing to impede him, even when she saw him bend over the living corpse. Andría did not sit down by the bed, but knelt on the carpet to get closer, as if to see Bonaria more clearly. Maria felt an impulse to go out and leave him alone but he intervened.

'Don't go,' he said, and it did not seem strange to either of them that he should be the one giving orders.

Maria said nothing but stayed standing by the door, while Andría silently watched the face of the *accabadora* of Soreni. She saw him stoop till his head was resting on the bedcover but without pressure, as though he were afraid of crushing the fragile body beneath it, a gesture of tenderness that revealed to Maria the part of him she thought she had lost. For a time they stayed like this, she standing watching, he breathing on his knees. Then Andría stood up and very lightly touched the comatose old woman's hand. Maria opened the door, and both went out, silent until they reached the front door.

'Thank you,' Andría said.

'It was nothing.' Maria surprised herself with her answer, disarmed by his gentle tone. 'If you'd like to come, some time . . . '

He shook his head.

'No, there's no point, all I needed was to see her like that. But if you need to go out, to get a bit of air . . . ' He interrupted himself, embarrassment fitting him like a glove. 'I mean, you know where I am.'

She gave him a smile, and when she went back into the house her heart was much less heavy. In some mysterious way related to his visit, the thought that had been eating her for weeks like a worm had pierced the threshold of potentiality, and become a clear decision. Going into the bedroom she found the pillow ready on the armchair beside the bed, picked it up and went closer, certain that this time no sense of guilt would stop her. Perhaps it was the gesture of tenderness she had seen in Andría that made her bend over Bonaria's face before acting, touching the old woman's cheek with a lightness she could not remember ever having felt before since she came home.

There are things one is absolutely certain of, and no evidence can do anything but confirm them; it was the sharp shadow of intuition that made Maria Listru certain that her mother, Bonaria Urrai, was dead.

★ ★ ★

In the days that followed, the whole village attended the funeral vigil of the *accabadora* of Soreni; not even those disabled in war stayed away from her funeral. Anna Teresa Listru made a constant display of a grief she most certainly did not feel, trusting in the wealth fallen into the hands of Maria, the daughter she now believed to have been transformed from her worst mistake into her best investment. On the other hand, every member of the Bastíu family wept for the dead woman

with sincere grief, while the priest Don Frantziscu Pisu desperately ransacked the twisted
depths of his feeble rhetoric in an attempt to
find acceptable words in which to avoid saying
that, in his opinion, the woman should not
even be buried in a consecrated churchyard.

Just as Bonaria had taught her, Maria
Listru Urrai wore her mourning with
discretion. Once Mass had been celebrated
on the seventh day and everything had been
performed correctly, Maria took Mosè and
went to fetch Andría. Together they walked as
far as the Pran'e boe vineyard, as far as the
stone structure that had been intended to fix
the altered boundary for once and for all. In
fact the stones had never been moved again,
yet nothing really seemed in its natural place.
Andría sat down on the wall, while Maria
sat on the ground with the dog beside her,
leaning back against the wall to look at the
vines, then closing her eyes in the sunlight.

Depending on the shifting direction of
the wind, the smell of cut stubble reached
them with varying intensity, while from high
in the sky came the cries of birds to whom
the sea beyond the hills was visible. The uneven
stones pressed against Maria's back and under
Andría, but neither seemed anxious to find a
more comfortable position. Then Maria leaped
deftly to her feet, and moving a few paces

raised her face to the breeze blowing from the sea as it caressed the vines in the valley. As the wind moved her dark skirt in an uncertain dance she breathed in, filling her lungs. Andría did not move but watched her in silence, then asked in a low voice:

'Now what will you do?'

'The only thing I know: dressmaking.'

'You'll stay here, you mean . . . '

'Have I ever gone away, Andrí?' she said, turning to look at him.

In her delicate profile he recognized something accomplished and familiar, and smiled. They had walked to the vineyard together, and together they returned home, totally undisturbed by the thought that they might be feeding the people of Soreni with even more idle gossip.